THE LATE MAN

ANDREAS SCHROEDER

THE LATE MAN

1972

𝔗𝔥𝔢 𝔖𝔬𝔫𝔬 𝔑𝔦𝔰 𝔓𝔯𝔢𝔰𝔰

Box 94, Port Clements, Queen Charlotte Islands, British Columbia, Canada

Designed and printed in Canada by
MORRISS PRINTING COMPANY LTD.
VICTORIA, BRITISH COLUMBIA

for adrianne

acknowledgements

Parts of *The Late Man* have appeared in the following literary journals:

The West Coast Review (Canada), *The Canadian Fiction Magazine* (Canada), *The Minnesota Review* (U.S.A.), *The Fiddlehead* (Canada), *The University of Windsor Review* (Canada), *Transformation* (England), D.N.A. — on ¼" magnetic tape — (Canada), *Beyond Baroque* (U.S.A.), *Scopcraeft* (U.S.A.), *Chelsea* (U.S.A.), *Outside Review* (England)

Acknowledgement is also made to:

Fourteen Stories High (Quarry-Oberon, 1971)
C.B.C. Radio: *Anthology*

The story of *The Late Man* has (with the financial assistance of the Canadian Development Corporation) been made into a 40-minute 16 mm. colour sound motion picture.
The written version here appears by courtesy of the Oberon Press, Ottawa.

contents

the late man

On the morning after the storm, the fishermen got up earlier than usual to survey the damage and repair what could be saved. Unusually strong winds and rain had scattered the nets and flattened gardens, bushes, even trees. Fishing boats lay strewn about the beach like broken teeth. Everywhere an exhausted silence hung limply; even the occasional seagull screech seemed blunted and uncertain. Across the mud-flats the faint rush of breakers seemed to fade, though the tide was coming in, slowly and without apparent conviction.

At this time in the morning the fishermen rarely spoke. They arranged their lines, oiled pulleys, checked over their engines and wordlessly pushed out to sea. To break the fragile silence of the first few hours would have been like bursting a delicate membrane without preparation; it was tacitly understood that a man needed more time to clear away in his mind the rubble and destruction of the preceding night, than was available to him between his getting up and the launching of his boat. Even after they had cleared the beach and set their course for the large fishing-grounds farther north, the fishermen rarely raised their voices — as if in instinctive respect for the precariousness of the human mind launched before sunrise on an uncertain sea.

11

But someone broke the silence that morning; as the last remaining boats poled into deeper water to lower their engines, a young bearded fisherman pointed to a single unattended boat lying on its side on the beach and asked in a low voice: "Where's he?"

The man being addressed looked startled, puzzled, then shrugged his shoulders.

The bearded fisherman risked a further offence. "Could he be sick, d'you think?"

There was no response. The other man slid his oar into the water and pushed them off.

*   *   *

A man opens his cabin door and steps into view. He is the late man, the man whose boat lies untouched on the beach below his cabin. There is nothing particularly unusual about this man except perhaps a certain slight hesitance in his manner; the hesitance of a man for whom the world became at some point intensely suspect, for whom, at that point, a glass on a table became less and less a glass on a table and more and more a thing too strange and amazing to grasp by name. As he stands in his doorway, his hand rests gingerly on the frame, as if constantly ready in case of attack.

About fifteen minutes have passed since the last boat was launched and the late man stepped from his cabin. Now, his boat ready and his outboard spluttering half-submerged, he pushes off and follows the fleet toward the fishing-grounds.

A few hours later the fishing village begins to yawn, stretch and get up; children and fishwives clutter the streets and tangle the air with punctuation marks.

*   *   *

When they return in the early evening and pull their boats out of the water above the high-tide markers, the late man is not with them. During the interval of time between the last fisherman's ascent from his stranded boat to his waiting dinner and the late man's arrival at the launching site fifteen minutes later, silence holds the breach like an indrawn breath. The sound of his prow on the pebbles, therefore, grates in an unusually harsh way on the nerves of the woman waiting for him above the high-tide markers. He has caught fewer fish than the other fishermen.

The next morning the late man appears at his cabin door half an hour after the fishermen have left the beach. Their boats are already vague in the distance when he finally manages to haul his boat to the water-line, which has by this time fallen far below his landing place with the receding tide. He seems somehow weakened, older, leaning wearily against the wheel of his boat. When the fishermen return that night he is an uncertain speck on the horizon, half an hour behind the last of the fishing fleet, and when the catch is scored, he has caught fewer fish than the day before.

*　*　*

Around noon the following day the boats were anchored in clusters to share both lunch and small-talk on the fishing-grounds, and the conversation turned to the late man. "Can't figure 'im out," one fisherman mused, pulling thoughtfully at his beard. "Won't tell nobody what's wrong." "Ain't sayin' a thing," another agreed. "Asked him yesterday what the problem was, but I'll be damned if he didn't seem like he wasn't even listening." There was a pause as if to let the spoken words disperse. Then: "Sea can do that to a man. Catches up with him, it does." The speaker slowly shook his head, threw an orange peel overboard, then absently ignored a deck-hand who had asked him what he meant. The deck-hand finally turned away, assuming his question was naive; he was new in the fleet and often found himself going unanswered. As it was, he was already on the other side of the boat when the old man muttered his answer to no one in particular: "I don't know what happens; I just know it does. Ain't no man can whirl the world by hand."

The next morning the late man launched his boat some forty-five minutes after the fleet had left the beach.

*　　*　　*

Little is known of the late man's history, though this is not realized until he first begins to attract attention by his mystifying dislocation of schedule; suddenly everyone rummages about in their memory for initial impressions, former opinions, latent suspicions, old predictions. Little in the way of substantial information is collected. It is generally agreed that he is a relatively young man, hard-working and "well-disciplined". Some felt him to be a little too much given to reflection, but one suspects this is said chiefly in reaction to his if not exactly anti-social, at least fairly reticent manner. He cares little for other people, though he has been known to go to the aid of a complete stranger for no reason. A slightly more observant villager notes his peculiar tendency to touch (with a curiously disbelieving air) whatever happens to be around him; the remark is received in uncertain silence. Many frankly admit they have no idea what to make of the whole business, and that the man is probably simply under the attack of some unsettling virus. This fails to explain, however (as someone quickly points out), his consistent, almost plan-like deceleration of pace in relation to the normal fishing schedule of the village

— by this time he is reported leaving the beach a full three hours after the last of the other boats has been launched.

*　*　*

By the time the late man pulls his boat from the water, the sun is little more than an almost-submerged leer on a mindless horizon and the waves have jelled to heavy, slowly swirling jibes. Night winds begin to cover the eastern part of the sky with a thick, cumulous ceiling of ridicule. Sardonic chuckles ripple along the water line where the undertow pursues an endless foreplay with beach gravel. The late man stands motionless, looking strangely as if he belongs neither to the water nor the land; his face is a ploughed field but his eyes dart about the beach like frightened piranhas. His boat is a crazily tilted sneer lying on its side in the pebbles, with rope dangling from the prow like corded spittle. Wave upon wave of curling laughter lampoons the beach. Everywhere, everything grins. The late man no longer defends himself. He has committed the blunder of allowing himself and the universe to discover his detective activities, his secret investigations into the nature and composition of himself and whatever he finds it possible to apprehend. But he has allowed this discovery prematurely, before he has had time to properly anaesthetize his specimens, and now, suddenly aware of a spy in their midst, they have disintegrated into countless labyrinthine possibilities and traps and the late man is cut off without the possibility of retreat. He has long since given up trying to sledge-hammer his brain to sleep.

But a violated universe will not be satisfied with the simple deflection of an inquisitive mind, and as if to make certain that such a trespassing will never again be possible, it has turned glaring spotlights against the late man's brain, blinding

15

and overwhelming it with confusion and derision. Stiffly aligned principles and corollaries suddenly go limp and begin to collapse; endless qualifications overrun simple premises and leave behind a shambles of tattered and useless shreds of belief. Above all, the horror is set creeping up the back stairs of the late man's mind that all this is beyond his control, and that like a retaining pin pulled from a spring-loaded wheel, this destruction will continue relentlessly until it has unrolled the tension from the spring.

There appears to be little he can do but to hold on until all is done, and to hope that he does not become so weakened in the process as to fall prey to a useless madness.

* * *

In a matter of months the departures and arrivals of the late man and the fishing fleet have diverged to such an extent that the returning fishermen see the late man's boat heading toward them at dusk, on its way north toward open water. He stands huddled over his wheel, eyes staring unseeing at the darkening horizon as if in purposeful blindness. The fishing fleet parts to let him pass; though no one appears to understand, everyone sees the desperate undertow in his eyes and says nothing. When all the boats are secured and the gear locked away, the late man is a dissolving blotch against black evening. A few moments later he is gone.

The late man had returned the previous morning with no fish at all.

As he sat down to dinner, the young fisherman who had asked about the late man early one morning suddenly spoke of him to his wife. "Nobody knows anything, or they won't say anything. Everybody pretends to ignore him. I've got to find out."

16

His wife said nothing. He looked at her curiously, then threw down his knife. "Well damn it, here's a man digging his own grave in plain view of a whole fishing village, and nobody has the guts to look into the matter." His wife remained silent but a worried look began to unsettle her face. The young fisherman stood up abruptly. "I'm going to find out," he said, reaching for his squall-jacket and opening the door. "Even if for no other reason than a simple matter of self-defence!" he added as the door slammed shut. Footsteps receded from the cabin. Within minutes the sound of his outboard began to move across the bay toward the fishing grounds and the open sea.

* * *

For a time the young fisherman directs his boat through thick total darkness; a bulging cloud cover muffles the moon and the night sways and sidesteps in ponderous movements that are blind but everywhere. The occasional clear splash falls short among the sluggish gurgle and sagging cough of deepwater waves beneath the keel. The young fisherman peers at the bleakness but steers his boat by instinct.

As he moves farther and farther into deeper water the night begins to thin out; his eyes detect edges, outlines, occasional glimpses of phosphoric glitter — eventually the moon disentangles from the clouds and trudges high into the sky, spraying a fine shower of thin light over the fishing grounds. By this time the young fisherman can make out the dark shape of the late man's boat, lying at anchor on his starboard side. The booms on the boat before him are out, trailing thin glistening lines into the water. The late man is fishing.

The young fisherman sits unmoving at his wheel, uncertain as to what should follow. Possibilities dart in and out of his

17

mind, unwilling to bite. He waits, his brain idling slowly, his thoughts loose.

A creak from a rusty tackle interrupts the silence. A glass-float dips and scrambles; the late man comes alive and begins to reel it in. A strike.

The young fisherman straightens up and strains to see. The glass-float tugs and splashes at the end of a stiff line; the late man's figure curves against the mast, his arms taut like two rigid claws shaking with exertion. The young fisherman feels an instinctive excitement thrill through his body as if the strike were his own. Something huge is on the end of that line.

The glass float is almost at boat's edge, momentarily calmer. The late man reaches for his fish-net and plunges it over the side, scooping carefully. His back is turned to the young fisherman, obscuring the float as he brings it to the boat's side. The fishnet rises from the water, then stops.

Surprised, the young fisherman leans forward but sees only the hunched back of the late man leaning over his net. A fierce rippling movement shakes the arm holding the handle as somethings twists and writhes in the meshes, but the late man makes no move to pull it into the boat. Ten minutes pass; the late man still stands bent over his net, gazing at his catch. The young fisherman is unable to see his face.

Finally, in a slow but deliberate movement, the late man empties his net into the sea and straightens up.

The young fisherman watches, still dumfounded, as the late man repeats the same procedure moments later when another line snaps alive. This time his demeanor seems to indicate recognition or less interest; a short look suffices to make him empty the net again. After a short pause a third float begins to bob and the late man reels it in. Half an hour later he is still engrossed in the net's contents, ignoring all the other lines

18

which are jerking at the boom. Bent over the gunwhale, his hair blowing about his head like spray in the wind, the man stares at his catch in silence, then throws it back into the sea.

*　　*　　*

As a faint paleness begins to tinge the outermost edges of the dark, the young fisherman stands up stiffly, a nervous flutter in his stomach, strangely excited yet uncertain why. He detects traces of the intoxication of discovery in his feelings, though he has no idea what he has discovered or realized.

Carefully pulling out his oars, he mounts them in the oar-locks and prepares to slip away. By the time the sun appears he will be back in the bay and his cabin. Then there will be time to think.

A small sound from the other boat stops his raised oars short. The late man has emptied his net and stepped back toward the mast. As he half-turns to re-apply bait to one of the lines the young fisherman catches a glimpse of the late man's face. He almost drops his oars.

The late man's face is totally disfigured. Crumbled skin, twitching lips and bleached white hair, he is suddenly old — an uncertain fool barely able to hold his balance in the rocking boat. The young fisherman is stunned. The late man was of the same generation as the others in the fishing fleet — chrono-logically about thirty years old. Now he looks three times that age.

But there is no time to lose; the horizon is becoming a thin pencil-line of light across the dark and he will be discovered. Stealthily moving his oars, the young fisherman pulls away toward the south and the fishing village.

As his boat moves into the bay, he sees the first cabin doors opening and fishermen walking down the beach toward their boats. Several of them look up, surprised to see his incoming boat at such an odd time. Obviously his wife has said nothing. He steers toward an unused part of the beach and runs his boat aground.

There, his boat bouncing slightly to the rhythm of his fading wash, he sat on the bow and twisted a piece of rope between his fingers; uncertain, almost nervous, uncertain again. The spreading sun warmed his back as he sat, but his stomach remained cold and unsettled; he felt the desperate urge to run, to commit a violence, tear something to shreds, but somehow he was numbed or simply unable to move. For no apparent reason something seemed to have snapped; his senses coiled and bunched in twisting knots, thoughts whirled in ever-tightening circles about his head and a steadily mounting pressure threatened to explode inside him like a surfacing deep-water fish.

Then the faint growl from a distant engine punctured the silence and the tension drained away with an almost audible hiss. The young fisherman looked over his shoulder and watched the late man's boat increase toward the bay. Several of the other fishermen paused and shaded their eyes. For a short while everything hung in suspension . . .

Suddenly the late man's boat is in the bay, its engine silent, drifting toward the beach. As its prow gouges into the sand the late man struggles feebly to climb off the deck onto the gravel, half-falling several times in the process. Then hoisting the bow rope over his shoulder, he attempts to pull his boat higher up onto the beach.

Later, after the late man had been buried and the fishermen had returned to their boats, the young fisherman was heard to say that in a totally paralyzed landscape, the only moving thing had been the late man trying to beach his boat. They had watched him for an incredibly long time, trying to raise the bow above the gravel, and when he finally collapsed, still no one had moved. When they eventually began to climb down toward the fallen figure, the landscape seemed to stretch and expand in every direction and they walked for hours before reaching him. They found him lying on his back, his face contorted with a mixture of agony and amazement; it was the oldest face they had ever seen. So they had buried him, quietly and without looking at each other, and the young fisherman had beached the boat. The next morning, due possibly to the tiring events of the preceding night and day, the young fisherman slept a little longer, and eventually launched his boat some fifteen minutes after the last of the fishing boats had cleared the bay.

the tree

He was an old man, though just how old was quite impossible to tell; he belonged to one of those aboriginal tribes whose members grow old at an early age and then seem to stop having anything to do with time at all. He was introduced to me simply as a "displacer of stones", a man who spent most of his time down at the beach lifting and replacing the jagged chunks of coral in search of whatever he could find. It was mentioned that his father had lowered the first fishing nets into the Macumba River.

He was an unperturbed old man, almost always smiling and nodding his head, trying to interest me in this or that triviality, often raising his calloused, almost black finger and delivering himself of little wisdoms which were translated to me as "People have more fun than anybody" and "In the days after the Great Heat, the heron sticks his legs into his pockets and flies elsewhere" or even the more unfathomable "In a land of little water, men weep less but take more women". Day after day I saw him wading along the beach at low tide, patiently turning over rocks, his fingers making quick darts into the water as whatever lurked beneath the stones blinked in the unaccustomed light and was caught. He dropped everything he apprehended into a smelly brown flour sack which he dragged into his hut at the end of the day, then lowered the curtain. I was never able to discover what he did with all he caught.

It was several weeks after I had met him that I was informed: "the old man has been told". At first I couldn't understand the information and no one seemed to understand my incomprehension, but eventually I discovered that the old man's death had been "officially forecast" by the tribal fortune-teller that day. After that there were no more smiles. When I saw the old man later that afternoon, his eyes gloomed and his face hung dully from his skull like his empty sack. He announced to me sadly that he would soon be turning into a tree; that the fortune-teller had divined his fate by looking at the seasons to come through the eyes of a dying rooster.

I asked if he knew exactly when this would occur, but he merely shook his head and muttered that "one would have to be careful where one stood from now on; one would have to be careful where one stood".

From that time on the old man became increasingly clumsy at displacing his stones; his attention was constantly divided between the water and the land, and he appeared always on the verge of making a dash for the line of trees just above the beach. Whenever he stopped to talk on the trail, villagers admonished him that "that is not a good place for a tree to stand", and he would hurriedly step aside among the bushes, continuing the conversation through the branches. His main concern was that when death became imminent, he would be able to reach an advantageous place where he could continue his life in tree form with relative comfort. For this reason he rarely dared to stray farther than a quick sprint away from such a spot.

Then the days began to grow longer and the tides receded farther from the land each day. Food grew more plentiful in the village and the fishermen risked deeper and deeper forays into the ocean's belly for sponge. Now, in the afternoons, the reef lay exposed for miles in every direction, baring an ever-increasing expanse of formerly concealed and mysterious sea-life. Every day saw the capture of new, colourful and obscure monstrosities which the villagers dried and added to their constantly growing string of temple gods. Only Katunga, the old displacer of stones, crouched near his tree-line and refused to hunt. The villagers made sympathetic, sorrowful clucking noises and brought the new spirits for him to see. Each time Katunga fingered the grotesque eyes and ornate scales of each new god, his eyes glowed darkly with the longing to join the search, as a displacer of stones should do. But he held grimly on beneath the trees, turning away.

It was one or two days after the kaantung, the Hottest Day, that I woke from my afternoon sleep to a frenzied shouting and clanging of pots through the village; children screamed, footfalls thudded rapidly past my curtain toward the beach, and everywhere I heard the name "Katunga". I pushed my curtain aside, the villagers pointed excitedly toward the reef and motioned me to hurry. Far across the treacherous maze of coral I saw a scattering of people straggling toward what appeared to be an unusually tall gaunt man flailing wildly about himself with his arms and legs.

"Katunga, Katunga" the villagers shouted, and as the tall gaunt man erupted into strange, jerking convulsions on the distant reef, I began to run.

As I jumped and stumbled across coral-encrusted boulders I remember thinking angrily, why couldn't he have resisted that temptation; should've stayed near the other trees where

25

he was safe, the damn fool, to go that far out has to be madness, and I almost rammed my foot down on a cluster of poison-filled spine coral and realized I was running much too fast for my own safety; when I looked up again he was already twice his original size.

I stopped. Katunga staggered as if jolted by enormous bursts of electricity, like a giant epileptic; what I had at first assumed to be reflections of his arms in the trembling heat were in fact many arms, some longer than others, some already very thick; his torso grew wider, heavier, rippling with straining, rebelling muscles; he was trying to run, to return, but his legs had already become too stiff to give him leverage and he tottered about until his feet entwined in the coral and anchored him fast. Above, his head disappeared in a burst of leafy green.

Now the transformation slowed, the struggle appeared resolved, the tree had asserted itself and the only movement I could still discern was the steady rising and unfolding of its crown, like the opening of a huge flower in the first rays of morning sun. A tentative breeze from the ocean riffled through the branches, swaying it slightly, and I thought for a moment I could still see Katunga trying to find more solid footing on the slippery reef, but that might have been only my imagination. By the time the first villagers arrived, they found nothing more than an implacable tree.

A dark tribesman standing next to me shook his head with a mixture of impatience and sadness. "This is not a good thing" he muttered, looking with some anxiety at the sky. "He has chosen a foolish place. Tonight the winds will be angry from the west, and the tides will leap high. He will drown."

I hooded my eyes and looked back at the strange tree of Katunga, standing improbably where in a few hours the ocean

would return and find him there, a giant plant in a sea-
meadow, clutching grimly to the rainbow molluscs and rub-
bery brain-coral underneath.

"He will be swept away" the tribesman muttered again. "It
was a foolish place, he does not know the sea; he will be swept
away."

the pub

To enter this pub we must pass through several doors, both of which are now being shouldered aside. The carpet flops limply, casually across the floor, around, under feet, table legs, fallen ashtrays and a broken cup. Various drinkers loll about the room, a woman laughs a little; friendly arguments here and there are stretched and tugged in and out of shape. Conversation splashes and drips, foams slightly.

It is warm here. The air billows gently against the ceiling and windows, unimportant, careless. A little of everything is everywhere, casually well-distributed, never enough to upset what it stands beside. The occasional shout pretends to tip the scales. There is little to remember here; little to keep in mind. We are here because there is little reason not to be. It is possible that this pub is very small.

What you must understand is that there is nothing unusual here. Everyone is well-worn, congenial; the furniture gently scarred, rounded — familiar to regulars and strangers alike. Light is spread like doilies across the chairs and tables before the bar. The waiter is fat, but not too fat. You will understand. There is an identical pub across the street.

A comfortable drone gurgles from the speakers of a brightly-lit juke box in the corner. Several couples dance. The pin-ball machine clicks and snaps; darts pock into the dart-board. And there: yes, the pay phones are all in use — regulars calling their friends to come on down: we're having a ball.

What makes a slightly unsettling noise is the coal hissing gently off-key behind the grate. The light may be somewhat uneasy here, flickering as it does behind bars. Under certain pressures glowing coal whistles thinly, like a faint suspicion. But this is easily explained.

Two couples sitting at a corner table have stopped talking, but they will soon begin again. The barman throws a glance over his shoulder and spills a little beer. He laughs. Spilling a little beer is a normal thing to do. The couple at the corner table notice this.

If the bricks around the fireplace are an angry red, it is because they have been recently painted, possibly to cover a smoke-blackened exterior. Excessive heat may cause the paint to peel, as it appears to be blistering directly above the flames. The mouth of the fireplace arcs in a pained frown.

A glass breaks. But the waiter denies this nervously, and upon closer inspection I must admit that it has only cracked. The couple in the far corner have not yet resumed their conversation, and there appears to be some doubt about their staying. The lady appears a little overwrought; undoubtedly they have had some petty disagreement.

Music spills from the corner juke box and those dancing step gingerly over and about the puddles of sound. The upturned chair near the center of the pub appears to have been accidentally knocked over by a man with a puzzled expression on his face. The unusual number of beer-glasses arrested in mid-movement from table to lips may have unnerved him; he gropes unsteadily for his chair but doesn't sit down.

The ragged end of the barman's towel flickers in and out about the bar furnishings like a snake's tongue. The only dart-player still engrossed in his game has just looked around; his missile flies wide of its mark, veers with a hollow bang into the old rubber tire encircling the dart board. A woman sitting near the spot where the dart drops to the floor jerks around with a small sharp cry.

Two men have begun to fumble with sudden twitching motions for their jackets. Pulling the coat from the back of his chair, one of the men knocks his beer-glass against an ashtray. Glass splinters fall endlessly to the floor. Identical sounds from another part of the pub may be due to a similar incident or simply an echo fracturing in the stunned silence.

A jagged rippling of movement jerks the drinkers about like puppets. A woman has begun to scream. The barman makes a movement toward her and another man snaps into motion like a spasm. There is the sound of a blow overlapping a terrified whimper. Blurred faces stretch, become a gaunt assortment of question/exclamation marks. Light hurls itself against a beer-tap, deflects, cascades across the counter foaming and hissing. Something bursts.

There is a hollow thud as enclosed spaces erupt. Wood cracks, metal screams out of shape and ruptures in all directions. Fists become hammers; shoulders, bulldozers. Everywhere, everything shifts, totters, gropes for collapse, until the shouts and blows tangle, weave madly in and out between the flailing arms and legs, soon quickly stiffen into a thick curtain and collapse. Darkness hardens to a rigid black. Sound only of dust drifting.

When the dust has settled, the damage is shaded in. Two chairs have been overturned, a table disarranged; two beer-glasses are cracked or broken and an ashtray chipped. The

31

barman stands rigidly behind his counter, rubbing a beer-tap senselessly, over and over again with jerky, idiot movements. No one moves anything anywhere; several people sit or stand about in impossible positions. A woman babbles quietly to herself in a far corner, facing the wall. Nothing is happening.

the painter

A wide empty beach; here, there, the beginnings of rock, of log. Light on light builds up to the thickness of day. The morning smells like fresh plaster. Slowly the empty window is shaded in; I stand, finally, and gaze out at nothing as yet; soon, a wide empty beach; here, there, the beginnings of rock, of log. Light on light builds up to the thickness of day. The morning smells like fresh plaster. Slowly the empty beach is shaded in; I sit, finally, at my easel and paint nothing as yet; soon, a wide empty beach, here, there, the beginnings of rock, of log. Light on light builds up to the thickness of day. The morning smells like fresh plaster.

* * *

At certain times, under certain atmospheric conditions, men have been known to see objects or locations hundreds of miles beyond the point at which the unassisted eye begins to fail. It is during such times, under such conditions that I have been known to see two painters, each within eyesight of each other, sitting before their easels at a cottage window and on an empty beach. It is possible that they are painting each other, or that they are painting themselves. They themselves, however, never appear in their paintings.

* * *

He was arriving when I first walked down to the beach to find a place for my easel. How long ago, I have no idea; I concentrate too closely on each individual consecutive day to enable me to maintain a sense of history in any but the most approximate form. We set up our easels simultaneously.

We set up our easels simultaneously. How long ago, I have no idea; I concentrate too closely on each individual consecutive day to enable me to maintain a sense of history in any but the most approximate form. He was walking down to the beach when I first arrived.

*   *   *

They paint exactly what they see, constantly. This requires unheard of quantities of oils, acrylics and lacquers which are brought to them ceaselessly by a great number of nondescript tourists and children. These tiptoe up to them from behind, tap them on the shoulder, and the painters pass over their right hands and take the offerings, then put them into baskets at their feet. They never turn around, and no one has ever dared to approach them from the front.

Often, when the weather is unsettled, when there are sudden changes of wind and cloud (this often occurs where the painters sit), they paint very rapidly, almost furiously; as a cloud shifts, they paint back the sky (or another cloud) into its place and paint it farther along, then move it again several minutes later. As the day begins to totter (days fall suddenly into nights where the painters sit) they dip more and more into greys, dusks and blacks until the canvas is totally darkened, then begin to break up the black with stars. Night is the most difficult time for the painters; it is only to the unpractised eye that the heavens are unmoving at that time. In reality there is ceaseless movement, an endless shifting of planets, meteors and

34

moons; it requires their utmost concentration to keep them all in mind and to track their orbits with their brushes. A mistake, an omission here forces them to admit disaster, and requires considerable amounts of yellows, reds, blues and greens to paint in the explosions, disintegrations and remains. And while they are so occupied they must nevertheless continue to follow the changes of the unaffected parts of the heavens or risk repetition of the collisions. It is possible that at times, on quiet nights, the painters purposely overlook some already wobbling planet and allow it to collide with another planet or sun. Painters, it is suspected, have a deep and secret love for fires.

*   *   *

I cannot say for certain, just how tired and bored a man must become to paint. Certainly when a man becomes too conscious of himself, and too conscious of being conscious, he breaks with a great laughter into Art. I have not always been a painter. But there was a woman who lived with me for many years before I realized I was painting. After the first year she began to change. One morning I woke and found her shoulders covered with a strange mercurial sheen; next morning it had spread to her neck and breasts. Neither of us ever discussed or even mentioned it. In the evenings we went to bed, made love, then put out the light . . . after that it was everyone for himself, trying to sleep.

It was not long before I became tired of the woman, or, more properly put, of us both. I needed something to entertain me. By that time, of course, I had been painting for some considerable time. I therefore invented the woman and began to paint what I saw in the reflections of her body.

*   *   *

A man sits before his easel in the cottage window. He has been there ever since I arrived, painting ceaselessly. He rarely moves, which saves me the work of painting his movements; I have little patience with objects or people who move slowly, forcing me to paint them in individual positions over and over again. The movements I insist upon are of sufficient velocity to appear as solid lines across the canvas — jagged, lean and black. This becomes impossible, of course, on hot days when the heat blurs the edges and bends cold straight lines into curves across an anvil sun. At such times it is not unusual for a woman to stumble inadvertantly into the landscape, disrupting the accumulated silence and forcing me to paint her every movement into the painting as she passes through, painting them all out again as she leaves. The woman also blocks my view of the painter in the window, and I am never sure after she has left, whether the man has moved while she was here. I have long suspected that he takes advantage of my inattention to move far more than I am later able to establish.

*　　*　　*

The two painters I have been known to see have been painting always. Layer upon layer of color, of oils applied with brush and pallet knife as the light spreads thickly across the day and bursts thinly into night. Soon there are so many layers of paint that the canvas will no longer stand in the easel and must be laid flat on the ground. As the thickness grows, higher and higher stools are required for the artists to reach the surface of their paintings. The shop coats of the artists grow mouldy and patches of moss cling to their shoulders and thighs. No one has ever seen them eating. More and more often disasters such as meteor and planet collisions occur; once a high tide, held back too long, bursts its outlines and floods the

36

entire canvas surface. The artist makes a creditable attempt to save the situation (so, at least, it appears), plunging his paint-filled brush again and again into the seething water to paint in dams, barriers and sand-bags — but to little avail, and when the tide recedes it washes away at least three years of work. For some unknown reason one of the painters suddenly falls off his stool and is unable to pull himself back into sitting position for three months, during which time all remains static, the rain which is not falling when the painter falls, continues not to fall throughout the three months, and many crops dry up and die.

It is possible that all this occurs as a result of passing time; however, it is equally possible that such disasters are effected intentionally by the artists. It is difficult to judge, for example, the degree to which the aforementioned physical descriptions of the painters are true; one can only confirm that men of such descriptions have appeared in the canvases of the two painters who are, possibly, painting each other.

*　　*　　*

Once, I suddenly realized that I was not there. I became quite frantic and began to dig down through the layers of paint in desperate search for even a single hazy image of my-self. I slipped off the stool and attacked the painting from the bottom. There was nothing. I became afraid that the painter on the beach might have moved in the interval and climbed back onto my stool. It is possible that he was climbing up his stool at the same time; when I looked at him, his face was red from exertion.

I became more and more dissatisfied. I was annoyed that, though it was I who was painting the landscape, the move-ments of trees, animals, stars, I was being excluded from my own painting. It was nothing short of intolerable. And all the while the painter on the beach appeared in it constantly, always; every morning I painted him emerging from the dawn mist, shaded him in, outlined him and painted him to work. And if he did the same to me, what good could it do me here, behind my cottage window at my easel?

*　*　*

The point at which a man begins to consider his exclusion varies; its occurrence, however, is inevitable, as is a consequent change of pace in the movement of events around and inside him. Suddenly a painter feels he realizes he has been excluded, though through whose fault or why is uncertain and quite possibly irrelevant. He decides to act. He realizes that to enter his own landscape is impossible, is suicidal, but this also is quite possibly irrelevant. He is proud to have managed to convince himself of something so ridiculous. . . .

They have left their easels and are walking toward each other. Possibly they will exchange places and assume authorship of their own existences in each other's paintings. Possibly, however, conditions will remain exactly as they were, regardless whether they exchange places or not. The latter possibility depends, of course, on what each individual painter wishes, or allows himself to believe.

A third possibility, contingent upon those already mentioned, is that the painters, after climbing onto each other's stools, look up and find themselves no longer there, having been (as you might imagine) painted out as they left their respective places. In which case we may assume suicide, effected in a way only artists can appreciate. The painting of the canvas, of course, continues as it would have continued in any case, regardless of the existence or nonexistence of the painters. . . .

the theft

It happened very quickly. I woke up, pushed myself out of bed, opened the bedroom door and walked smack into a tall, fat man leaning against my bookshelf. We looked at each other enquiringly.

"You might be a little more careful," he reproached me gently. "You've spilled my coffee quite unnecessarily." He was drinking from one of my stoneware mugs.

"And what the hell might you be doing in my living-room?" I threw back, not quite awake, but already beginning to flare like a struck match. His companion, a younger, slighter man with wire-rimmed glasses, came out of my study at the sound of my voice.

The living-room was littered with papers, pens, bottles of drawing inks, advertising copy and construction-paper fold-outs. Obviously they had been working for some time.

"Is that your trash all over the room?" I flung at them, stabbing a threatening finger through the air and toward the tall fat man. His face seemed made of listless rubber.

"It is," he admitted, sounding mildly surprised. I stooped and swept a stack of papers from the table. "Then get it out!" I snapped, indicating the door. "And don't forget to include yourself!"

"I said get the hell out!" I boiled over, when both just stood there looking puzzled. "Take your garbage and yourselves and beat it!"

The younger slighter man cleared his throat: "Beat it?" he asked in a faintly perplexed tone; "I don't think you understand. We've come for our things."

"Excellent, excellent," I dumped at his feet; "What a thoroughly delightful coincidence we both agree. Only next time, you might have the courtesy to use someone else's apartment for whatever you're doing." I slammed the bedroom door.

When I had dressed and re-opened the door, I saw the tall fat man handing an armful of my books to the younger, slighter one. A surge of incredulous fury splashed across my brain. "Are you out of your skull?" I yelled. "What in blazes are you doing with my books?!"

"*Your* books?" the tall fat man demanded softly. I grabbed a large leatherbound volume I had owned for years and slapped open the cover to show him my name on the inside. There was no label. "Next page," the tall fat man suggested. I flipped the page. The name I read was L. Benson Karwinkel. That was not my name.

"I'm Benson Karwinkel," the tall fat man introduced himself quietly. "This is my friend Leonard Briggs." The younger, slighter man put down the lamp he had unplugged and nodded pleasantly.

"Well you can damn well put down my lamp, Mr. Leonard Briggs," I snarled, furious and mystified at the mix-up about the books. "I'll thank you to leave my furniture just where it is."

Mr. Leonard Briggs wordlessly raised the base of the lamp toward my face. *Property of Benson Karwinkel* I read engraved in the metal. The tall fat man was heading for my type-writer.

My brain went into a slow spin, circling warily, trying to find the exit, the culprit; to determine and define the enemy. The tall, fat man was carrying off my typewriter. I could see BENSON KARWINKEL in raised letters on its side.

I pulled my camera out from under the coffee table and looked at its underside. *Property of Benson Karwinkel.* This was going too far. I'd had enough.

"The next sonofabitch who touches a single piece of my property," I threatened, clenching my fist under the tall fat man's nose, "gets it right between the eyes. I don't know what your game is and how you've managed this, but you're not going to pull it off, I assure you!"

The tall fat man's face seemed made of a listless rubber.

"Game?" the younger slighter man queried gently, setting the typewriter down at the door. "You did advise that we take our things and go."

"I'm not going to waste time arguing about it," I hammered out; "You take precisely what's yours and not a thing more; grab a single thing of mine and I'll split your head!"

The tall fat man cleared his throat. "These things of yours have my name on them," he pointed out calmly. "Are you sure they belong to you?"

He picked up my briefcase and pointed at the tag. L. BENSON KARWINKEL.

"Look, I'm sure you've got this all worked out," I became frustrated; "My lines and your lines; but I warn you; I haven't learned my part and I'm not playing. Just get out of my house!"

"I think you've stolen all these things," the tall fat man continued mildly; "I've been wondering where many of my possessions have been disappearing to. This may explain everything."

"Oh come now, I'm sure you can do better than that," I sneered. "It's hardly likely; I've never seen you in my life."

"Take the man's wallet, Leonard," the tall fat man ignored me. "Let's have a bit of a look at it."

"The first sonofabitch . . . " I began, but hardly had time to clinch with the man before I found I was dealing with a professional. My wallet lay in the hand of the tall fat man.

"You see what I mean," he turned to me slowly, pulling out my papers and cards. Driver's license, credit cards, press pass, passport, birth certificate. "All these cards are mine," he accused, a faint tinge of hostility darkening his voice. "L. BENSON KARWINKEL. My name on every one."

"You rotten crook!" I hissed, struggling against the younger, slighter man's grip. "They're mine. I applied and paid for every one. I don't know how your name got onto them, but they're not yours, and you know it."

"You stole them," the tall fat man nodded, unruffled. "I didn't want to make a theatrical episode out of all this, and I still don't. We'll leave, as you suggested, with our things. Tie him up for the time being, would you Leonard; I don't want any more scenes."

I watched them carrying everything out. Each time they picked up an object, they held it in front of my face to show the name. They emptied the entire apartment.

When the last piece of furniture had been taken away and the rug rolled up, the tall fat man stuck his head back through the door and said, his voice echoing strangely in the naked, hollow room: "I don't know what prompts me to this bit of kindness, but I'm leaving you the apartment. I don't have to, you know; the lease is in my name."

42

the roller rink

I will admit at the very outset of the following history that parts of it may be untrue. Unfortunately, I can no longer tell which parts — I have been reworking these notes for such a long time now that my own fabricated sections have become indistinguishably blended with the original facts. I am not even certain precisely how I first stumbled into the environs of the story, though I seem to recall it was while I was stranded in a small village in southern Germany many years ago. I remember nursing a particularly vicious headache at the time and attending to several impressive bruises (unfortunately I have no idea where I might have sustained these knocks) when, for some reason, I noticed a long, oval building standing fairly far back from the street. There was a jagged hole broken through one of its walls.

Normally I wouldn't have paid much attention, but directly below the hole I saw the imprint of a body which presumably had fallen through the hole and lain for some time on the grass below. From the hole itself I could hear the smooth rush of countless ball-bearinged wheels against a background of lilting electric organ music.

* * *

The oval building was a Roller Rink, and a very popular one it appeared, for when I approached the front booth for my ticket I was given a card indicating my application had been noted and instructing me to take a room in one of the nearby hotels until my turn came up. I took a room as directed and settled in for a wait which lasted many months and often threatened to drive me quite mad with boredom, had I not had the company of others who were also waiting to take their turn. I soon discovered that virtually the entire village was comprised of hotels and boarding houses, all of which were constantly filled to capacity with persons waiting to be admitted into the Rink.

After almost three seasons had passed, an errand boy brought the message that I was to present myself the following morning at the front ticket booth to complete certain formalities prerequisite to my entry into the hall. I spent that night with my waiting companions celebrating the good news, accepting the tearful goodbyes and good wishes accorded those about to take their turn. In the morning, after a hurried breakfast, I paid my bill and headed for the Rink.

My excitement was such by this time that I paid scant attention to the "formalities" and am consequently unable to reproduce them here, but I do remember being ushered assiduously into the Dressing Room, a large, high-ceilinged, almost clinical looking chamber with white walls and a bevy of brisk girls in white smocks always available to help newcomers into their skates.

My enquiries about the hole in the wall — my initial reason for seeking entry into the Rink — were politely but firmly ignored, and I was entreated to hurry with the putting on of my skates to make room for others who had waited as long as I and were understandably impatient. I realized there was little

44

I could do for the present and decided therefore to have a closer look at the hole once I was mobile and able to inspect this mystery on my own.

*   *   *

To maintain one's balance in this Rink implied learning to skate from scratch, regardless of any former skating experience, and irrespective of the skater's age or native abilities.

At first, people landed on their knees, slid about on their backsides or completely disappeared; others, though not immediately recognizable as themselves, suddenly flickered into view and bounced heavily across my vision. At times, then more and more often, they struggled by, eventually streaked by, pieces of wall stood firmly for a moment, then glanced away hesitantly, soon casually, and I began to lose sight of the individual boards and sections of rail. Later, possibly much later, people receded swiftly in perspective, about-faced, dipped and rolled smoothly away, and the business of maintaining my balance became a matter of personal, not public, survival.

By the time I was secure enough on my feet to think about destinations, many more months had passed, and I had almost forgotten what I had entered the Rink to find. Almost as an afterthought, one day, I set course for the far wall where I had seen the hole.

*   *   *

The hole was not there. The hole was no longer there. There was no hole. There had never been a hole broken through the wall of this Roller Rink.

Standing against the railing alongside the wall, I couldn't decide which statement was the true explanation for what I couldn't find. A long, smoothly dove-tailed, highly varnished

45

barrier receded unbroken into the distance, where it curved slightly and disappeared. Wherever it might have been, the hole was no longer anywhere in evidence.

Though I was badly disappointed with this conclusion, there seemed to be little I could do to change it. Standing as I was on the edge of the main stream of traffic, I suffered several near-accidents as the skaters, unaccustomed to stopping or circumnavigating others who had stopped, collided with me from behind and nearly pulled me down. I soon realized that stopping virtually anywhere on the course was extremely dangerous, and that the safest thing was to keep moving at a steady, moderate rate, regardless of any irregularities which aroused my curiosity. This way, at least, there tended to be no surprises.

Of the following dozen years there is little to tell. I skated incessantly, round and round the enormous oval hall, gradually losing all sense of a time before my entry into the Rink. From the continual circling I developed a mild but perpetual dizziness which dulled the senses in a peculiarly pleasant sort of way, so that I stopped even my formerly habitual jotting down of notes. There seemed little point to it after all; what minor changes occurred in the daily routine were hardly sufficient to warrant mention.

Not that my subsequent life became completely uneventful; there were enough clashes and quarrels with other skaters to provide an often disagreeable overtone to my life in the Rink. Most of squabbles occurred when I began to tire of the persistently monotonous pace and attempted to skate in reverse or engage in a little racing. Invariably, the ripples of indignation and even fear which passed through the crowd soon forced me to re-align myself in the proper manner and subside. The skaters clung to each other timidly, carefully balancing their

46

proprieties before themselves in sober ritual. Confrontations for any reason whatsoever were considered entirely unacceptable. Instead, the singing of hymns and patriotic songs was encouraged, effectively masking the sounds of argument or dispute.

*   *   *

In retrospect, now, I doubt that I would have lasted many more years in that Rink had I not been offered, by the Rink directors, a course in roller rink management. I was informed that, though my rebelliousness has compromised my position to some extent, the directors were willing to consider the past a period of adjustment, and that I would be given this unusual chance to redeem myself.

My studies would encompass the entire area of skate mechanics, the styles and techniques of the skill, the different types of music and their effects on the skating masses, also designs of rinks, the various kinds of flooring, different brands of varnish, paint, leather padding and the variety of layouts available for lobby and rest areas. I was to study the arts of timing and pacing, the various rhythms, the tension of centrifugal and gravitational forces played off against one another for balance; in short, the entire problem of the man on wheels.

Though I balked somewhat at the tone of the offer I decided to accept, realizing that I had been in the Rink too long to remember how to survive elsewhere, and hoping this would make my life in the Rink a little more interesting or at least endurable. Under diligent direction I began to spend hours every day repairing torn buckles and straps, replacing lost bearings, exchanging worn wheels and tightening loose or damaged screws. With my manual in one pocket and a small set of portable tools in the other, I spent whole weeks cruising

47

the skating floor, helping hapless skaters who had run into difficulties. As time passed I worked with increasing desperation, feeling always on the edge of disillusionment, always on the verge of betrayal, hoping somehow that a deeper involvement would result in a more secure commitment to the idea of the Rink itself. For when I stopped to think about it, I could feel it slipping from my grasp like a smooth round elusive stone, the belief in the skaters, the Rink, the skating round and round the interminable oval, the never-ending repairs to equipment which stumbled along for a short while, then collapsed again. It began to make less and less sense to me how I could have abandoned all that I had been before (though I had to admit I could no longer remember with any certainty just what I had been) with little more than a shrug of the shoulders and a vague curiosity about a hole in a wall which I couldn't even locate anymore.

The more I realized this, the more I tried to smother my uneasiness in additional work, driving myself with a fiercely clenched mind, deeper and deeper into the tendrils of a vocation leading to Supervisor of Those Who Skate.

When, ten years later, I had chased myself through the entire course, I took up my post as administrator of the large, well-worn Rink and settled in for a term of helping the skaters through their paces.

The Rink, by this time, had been growing too small for my taste and I made immediate application for permission to undertake major renovations throughout the hall. There was bickering, grumbling, and much frustrating pedantry, but the permission eventually materialized and the work was launched. By spring of the following year the renovations were almost complete, with work going on solely in the main rink of the skating complex. This area was, as you might imagine, my special concern.

Through my studies I had begun to realize that the secret to a happy congregation and a long-lasting Rink was to position its walls in such a way as to make the skater believe he is moving constantly in a straight line. With this in mind I laboured long hours over the walls and floor to ensure absolute smoothness and continuity. As I sanded and polished each board again and again, it seemed to me that I was not only smoothing the way for others, but straightening the compromising curvature out of my own life.

When the renovations were entirely completed several weeks later, a great inauguration celebration was proposed.

It was decided we would begin the ceremony by all skating once over the entire area of the Rink. At the signal of the juke box operator (who had recorded a new piece of music designed especially with the new walls in mind) we would begin, with myself in front and the whole skating pack following in neat, orderly rows behind.

The planned celebration was to last throughout an entire week and drew much attention and excitement among the masses which gathered in the Rink lobby on the first day of the feast. It took much effort to prod the entire crowd into its correct position for the beginning of the journey; confused skaters stumbled about everywhere, falling against railings, losing their balance to crash into already assembled lines which promptly lost their cohesion; there was much quibbling over which rows were the most desirable and who should warrant skating where. When everyone was finally in his place, I raised my hand and waved for silence.

The juke box operator gave the sign. Smoothly, as if driven by electricity, I glided off, pulling my assistant supervisor after

49

me. Row after row set off, until soon the entire herd was in motion, swaying leisurely, easily, from foot to foot to foot. Old women smiled at old men who grinned and nudged each other playfully; the atmosphere was high-spirited, contented and free.

A little time passed. I began to increase the pace bit by bit; the floor was so smooth and the wall so continuous, there was nothing by which anyone could gauge their speed — so there were no complaints. I tried to count the boards in the wall to keep track of our progress but we were soon skating so fast that the boards blurred as we rolled by and I found it difficult to decide where one board ended and the next began. Someone behind me had begun a hymn; I remember being annoyed for an instant that someone should have started the singing without my prior consent, but there was no sense in making a scene on such a special occasion and, besides, we were now speeding along at such a rate that my turning around would have meant placing the balance of the entire skating assemblage in jeopardy.

Suddenly, I thought I felt myself beginning to edge very slowly toward the right, toward the wall. Surprised, uneasy, I looked down at my skates; everything seemed in order, the wheels were spinning along quietly, the leather straps were tight and the metal clamps for the toes seemed secure. It was when I pushed a little harder with my right leg in an attempt to reposition myself into my former place, that I heard the click. It sounded as if a bearing had chipped.

Puzzled, I looked up to see that I was still moving very slowly toward the wall. Trying to ignore the noise in the bearings (which was becoming more and more pronounced) I strained once again toward the left. My skates resolutely refused to shift — and suddenly it dawned on me that we had reached that section of the wall at which the curve began.

I turned my head, glanced back — nothing but elation, singing, horseplay — no one noticed the drift of the curve.

A flood of anger, exasperation and resentment poured through my mind as I began to realize the implications of this trap, but there was no longer time for thought; I struggled bitterly now, closer and closer to the speeding wall; my skates making a terrific racket but everyone singing so loudly that no one could hear. My eyes began to hurt; I saw nothing but smooth continuous boards streaking past my pupils back into my skull — stooped down in a grasping effort to undo my straps, thinking possibly to leap out of them, more image than idea — a split-second later I felt my shoulder brush the wall, my right skate screamed along the varnish, dug in, my body swung around and slammed into the wall, I saw an enormous blackness and then there was nothing . . .

*   *   *

Total silence. Or a gentle hissing sound around the edges of a hole which may not even be an exit, which possibly exists in outline only, in the imagination of a skater just escaped into the confines of a larger surrounding rink. There is room for argument of course, and some evidence that there was, in fact, an actual hole. But it may perhaps be appropriate to point out that it is not as uncommon a thing as it might appear, for a man to construct his past in ramp-like fashion to launch himself into a future he might not otherwise be able to afford. It is possible, for instance, that this gaping story is itself the hole through which the man in question fell, or that it is a substitute for the hole he never found. Another possibility may be arrived at by superimposing the identities of the man at the beginning and the man at the end, placing them on opposite poles of the story's own oval configuration.

Of course it may be that none of these possibilities apply, being suggested, as they are, by the author himself who has admitted from the beginning that an undeterminable part of this fiction may have been fabricated and therefore be untrue. For one thing, it must be pointed out that such feinting is characteristic by persons attempting to make good an escape by confusing their pursuers with false leads and half-true information. But of course this warning, too, is suspect, having been made by the presumed escapee himself . . .

the connection

IIIIIIIIIIIIIIIIIIIIIIIIIIIIIIIIIIIIIIIIIIIIIIIIIIIIIIIIIIIIIIIIIIIIIIIIIIIIIIIIIIIIIIIIIIIIIII

1.

"This is your air ticket and this, as you see, your health certificate. Car reservations have been made for you at your destination, and of course hotel arrangements as well." The secretary speaks in a brisk, confident voice, laying various documents on the desk before one Mr. Derringer, recently-hired employee of a well-established oil company in the Northwest. Derringer murmurs his thanks, double-checks several items on his itinerary, picks up his briefcase and departs.

When the plane touches down at New York's Kennedy Airport, Derringer gathers his belongings, shrugs on his overcoat and prepares to meet the public relations man who is to fill him in on missing details. As he picks his way down the ramp stairs, a stewardess calls his name.

"Mr. Derringe!" "Mr. Derringe of Chicago!" Derringer makes himself known. "Derringer," he corrects. "Derringer, with an *r*." The stewardess glances at a piece of paper in her hand and shrugs. "A message for you Mr. Derringe," she monotones. "Please check with the Passenger Information counter on the Departures level."

Derringer frowns as he rises up the escalator to Departures. There is supposed to be a company man here. At Passenger Information a young girl searches through her files. "Mr. Derring? That's you? Yes, I have a message here that you're to fly on to Florida. A change in plans." She holds out an air ticket for him to sign. "The name's spelled wrong," Derringer notes. "My name ends in *er*."

"Oh dear, I'd better check this," the girl worries, re-thumbing through her files. "Ah here we are; Mr. Dorrengor right?" "Not quite," Derringer replies. "*er* you know; *e* as in elphinstone, *r* as in rape." The girl lays both tickets on the counter; the second is for Mexico.

"I'd suggest you better decide which refers to you Mr. Dorrengor," she says. "The plane for Mexico leaves in ten minutes, and the one for Florida in twenty-seven. We've got to reroute your luggage, you know." She sounds somehow reproachful.

Derringer feels annoyed and undecided. He has no idea whom he might phone for help; it is now Sunday and no one would be reachable anyway. He chooses Dorrengor, signs the ticket and has the tags on his suitcase changed. In a short time he is on his way to Torreon, Mexico.

2.

A stewardess in Torreon is expecting him. "Mr. Farronga?" she asks politely as he steps from the plane. "Your car is waiting for you on Level 5." "You've got the name wrong again," Dorrengor informs her, tired and irritated. "Then this doesn't apply to you?" the stewardess queries apologetically. "I'm so sorry." The flight passengers disperse, the stewardess circulating among them inquiring "Farronga?" of every man she sees.

No one answers to the name. When all the passengers have departed, Dorrengor and the stewardess are left behind. "I suppose that message is for me," he decides, and has his luggage brought to Level 5.

3.

"You're Mr. Fatronca?" the rental agent asks. "Sign here, please." Farronga signs. The agent hesitates. "The signature doesn't match the name," he points out. "I can't possibly let a car go out with a descrepancy like that."

Farronga reflects. He has a choice of bogging down at this point or ploughing on, possibly saving a lot of time. "It's spelled differently in different countries, of course," he snaps at the agent. "Here; if it's so important to you, I'll spell it your way."

The agent looks relieved and checks the papers again. "You can simply leave it at the Sao Santos Airport when you arrive there, Mr. Fatronca," he offers. "We'll send a man to pick it up. The guy who rented the car for you didn't say when your flight was due to leave, but they generally depart in the afternoon there." Fatronca thanks him with a wave of his hand and enters the elevator for the carpark.

4.

The airport is relatively small, serving less than half a dozen airlines, many of them local. Farronga checks with each ticket counter but no one recognizes his name. Eventually, hungry and frustrated, he heads for a coffee bar for breakfast. Suddenly the P.A. system pages a Mr. Garroncton, flying to Peru.

Fatronca mulls over the name; there is a possibility, he

55

thinks. He walks to the airline counter in question and answers the page. The airline agent agrees that the name is certainly not the same, but produces a photograph he has been given to identify the expected passenger. Though the similarity with Fatronca is doubtful, there is enough resemblance for the agent to ignore the dissimilarities. He hands Garrincton his ticket and wishes him a comfortable flight.

5.

The aircraft is a rattling old DC-3, a 37 passenger capacity propellor plane with only a handful of people on board. Garroncton suddenly realizes he doesn't even know his specific destination and rings for a stewardess to ask. He is informed the aircraft is flying to Sicuani, Peru, expecting to land there in about five hours time. Garroncton settles back in his seat and waits.

The service is poor, passengers are served only a cup of coffee and two plastic-wrapped cookies during the entire flight, and it seems to Garroncton the service has been becoming increasingly unsatisfactory since his departure from Chicago some days ago. His complaint merely produces two more plastic-wrapped cookies, however, and he gives up the fight. Nobody else seems to care in any case; most other passengers are either asleep or lazily browsing through magazines.

They land at Sicuani Airport in the thick fog of early morning, the aircraft bumping uncomfortably along the badly patched runway to a cluster of miserable little buildings on the northeast corner of the airfield. The half-dozen passengers quickly disperse and Garroncton is left standing helplessly in the middle of the building, quite at a loss as to how to proceed. A check of the two ticket offices produces nothing; no one

appears to be expecting anyone by a name even faintly re-
sembling his own. The cafeteria is closed, an old cleaning
woman pushes her mop up and down the floor, the clatter of
her wash-pail echoing emptily in the deserted hall.

6.

Garroncton sits on his suitcase in the middle of the floor and
tries to take stock of the situation. He thinks of one possibility,
then another, but every thought seems to end in the feeling
that he's got to get out of here, keep moving toward where
he's expected, where a company man can fill him in on the
missing details. Maybe this is some sort of test of his stamina,
his imagination, his inventiveness. Besides, he thinks he remem-
bers the company man who interviewed him saying they had
interests in Peruvian oil.

His reverie is interrupted by the slam of a swinging door.
Garroncton looks up to see a leather-clad, heavily bearded man
standing in the doorway, looking up and down the hall. He
swings a pair of goggles absent-mindedly from his left wrist.
There being no one else in the hall, the man approaches
Garroncton.

7.

"Your name Garotta by any chance?" he asks Garroncton in
broken English. Garroncton hesitates. If he admits to the dis-
crepancy in the name he might end up stuck in this crumbling
hole for days. Besides, the name isn't that far off. He nods at
the bearded man. "Yeah, that's me I guess. What've you got
for me?"

The man in the leather jacket shrugs. "Supposed to take you

57

to Cocama, far as I know," he says. "That sound right to you?" Garotta tries to look informed. "Sounds like the place," he returns. "Here's my suitcase and grip."

They walk out to a peeling, oil-streaked Aztec standing like a forlorn insect on the far end of the runway. The pilot looks at the suitcase critically. "'M afraid we're gonna have to leave that here," he informs Garotta, shrugging his shoulders with a grimace. "Not enough room in this old heap for us and that thing too. Somebody else gonna have to bring it later." Garotta says nothing. The engines spit and wheeze for some seconds, then splutter into life, the little plane shaking as if it had suddenly contacted Parkinson's Disease. The pilot pulls back on the throttle.

Once airborne, they clamber shakily to 3000 feet, the aircraft dipping and slewing like an uncertain dragonfly. The pilot shouts something which Garotta fails to understand over the noise, then both concentrate on looking ahead at the eery cloud forest through which the aircraft navigates.

As they break clear of the clouds an hour later, Garotta sees a sparse sprinkling of glittering buildings far below, tucked in at the foot of the mountain range dead ahead. The pilot sets the plane about in a steep bank, plummeting down between two peaks toward the valley where Garotta now makes out the faint X pattern of the runway. Five minutes later they bounce down on the close-shorn grass of the tiny airstrip and roll the plane to a halt. There is no sign of life anywhere.

A small herd of goats stampede from the side of the strip as Garotta jumps off the wing of the Aztec and looks around. "I'll get someone to deliver your bag eventually," the pilot shouts, not leaving his seat. "It may take a while." "Hold on!" Garotta commands, somewhat alarmed. "Where's the company man who's supposed to meet me here? The guy who's supposed to fill me in on missing details." "Company man," the pilot shouts back. "Never heard of a company man. Nobody ever meets anyone here. Not on my flights anyway." The last words are almost drowned out by the increased roar of the engines. The pilot shouts something else which Garotta can no longer hear, guns the engine and taxis down the strip. A few moments later he is only a receding speck in the vast, blue sky.

8.

Garotta sits down on the grass, almost dazed; around him, strange birds warble and chirp like bursting bubbles or electronic static. The buildings at the corner of the field are abandoned; he can't find a soul anywhere. Two days later finds him eating berries from bushes around the airstrip to keep alive, waiting for the Aztec to return.

9.

The following day a dusty, haggard-looking native creaks onto the field in a dilapidated donkey cart. "You Sēnor Tarotina?" he quavers, squinting at Garotta in the sun. Tarotina nods and climbs into the cart. "We are going . . . " the native explains and cracks his long, frayed whip.

the freeway

For a long time: nothing but the hiss and whine of tires on pavement. A faint growl from the exhaust. Occasionally, querulous squeaks of springs and loose screws as the vehicle jounces over dips and bumps in the road. Finally:

MAGDA: *(fretfully)* Grandfather!

GRAND: What's wrong, Magda?

MAGDA: Grandfather, it's so dark outside. Where exactly are we?

GRAND: Just passing through the canyon, child.

MAGDA: The canyon?

GRAND: That's right.

MAGDA: I don't want to drive in this old car anymore, Grandfather.

GRAND: Don't be impatient, my dear. We're getting there.

MAGDA: But we're going so slow, and my seat is tired.

GRAND: Think of the city, child. We'll be there in a few hours.

MAGDA: In this old thing?

GRAND: It's taking us where we're going, Magda. Besides, I own it.

MAGDA: *(grumpily)* Well it sure isn't very comfortable.

GRAND: I don't think that's particularly important. It's getting there that counts.

Along the long, narrow freeway, the asphalt stretches from north to south like two thin black arms whose hands are hooked limply over the rails of the opposing horizons. Vehicles scurry along the black path like mechanized rats with huge eyes and often bared, rigid teeth.

MAGDA: Look, Grandfather! A beautiful shiny bus, I'll bet it's brand new.

GRAND: It's very full.

MAGDA: Look at all those kids, waving their arms around. They're singing, they're having a good time.

GRAND: There's nothing much else to do on a bus.

MAGDA: I'd sure like to ride in one of those. Why don't we ever take a bus, Grandfather?

GRAND: A man's got to have control of his own four wheels. There doesn't seem to be much point, otherwise.

MAGDA: Well I'd sure rather ride in a shiny bus than in this rickety old car.

GRAND: You've never ridden in a bus before, Magda; you don't know what you're talking about. Buses don't give you much of a choice in anything; you either adapt your departures and destinations to their schedule, or you walk.

MAGDA: I don't mind.

GRAND: You would if you ever took a ride in one.

MAGDA: Well why don't we take a train then?

GRAND: That should be pretty obvious. Why don't we take a train?

MAGDA: *(grudgingly)* I guess you mean on account of the rails and all that stuff.

GRAND: Of course.

MAGDA: What about airplanes though? They can turn anytime they want.

GRAND: That's true, but they can only land in specific places. They can't just stop anywhere, anytime.

MAGDA: *(frustrated)* Well OK, maybe that's all true, but I'm still really tired of this old car.

GRAND: Keep your mind on the city, Magda; you've spent so much time looking forward to it and now you seem to be forgetting all about it.

MAGDA: But it's all taking so awfully long. *(querulously)* How far is it now?

GRAND: About 40 miles I should think; there should be a sign coming up pretty soon . . .

The old man increases his speed a little as the sedan moves into a curve and begins to lean heavily against its two left wheels. The young girl pulls herself firmly against the door to avoid sliding into her grandfather along the seat. Suddenly she points toward the roadside several hundred feet up ahead:

MAGDA: Hey, there's the sign! *(reads)* "40 MILES TO REVELL RIVER"

GRAND: *(leaning forward against the window)* Where? Where can you see a sign?

MAGDA: *(a little anxious)* There, right ahead. In the curve.

GRAND: That's odd; I can't seem to . . .

MAGDA: *(alarmed)* You're heading straight for it, Grandfather! What're you doing? Look out!

GRAND: I can't see it! I just can't seem to . . .

With a hollow popping of gravel and squeals of rubber, the back end of the old sedan breaks away, fish-tailing across the

63

road and slamming with a heavy thud into the opposite ditch. An exclamation of steam erupts from the radiator grill; doors burst open and slam against the sedan body, showering flakes of paint. Air hisses from two ruptured tires.

When the noise of the crash has subsided:

MAGDA: Grandfather! Grandfather, are you OK?
GRAND: I don't know child. Sometimes I just don't know.

*   *   *

For a long time: nothing but the hiss and whine of tires on pavement. A faint growl from the exhaust. Occasionally, querulous squeaks of springs and loose screws as the vehicle jounces over dips and bumps in the road.

Finally:

MAGDA: We didn't do so well that time, did we Grandfather?
GRAND: It could have been worse. How did you manage?
MAGDA: I think I broke my leg. It'll be hard walking.
GRAND: Well, you won't really have to; we drive most of the time.
MAGDA: All of the time, Grandfather.
GRAND: Now Magda, I've told you not to talk like that. We'll get there. Pretty soon now.
MAGDA: Hmm.
GRAND: We will, believe me. I only lost two fingers this time.
MAGDA: Can you still drive all right?
GRAND: Of course I can drive.

Along the long, narrow freeway, the asphalt stretches from north to south like two thin black arms whose hands are hooked limply over the rails of the opposing horizon. Vehicles scurry along the black path like mechanized rats with huge eyes and often bared, rigid teeth.

MAGDA: Shall I sing for you, Grandfather?

GRAND: I can't understand singing, child. I only understand the music of engines.

MAGDA: Have you had many cars, Grandfather?

GRAND: Of course.

MAGDA: More than there were on that old wrecker's yard we passed yesterday?

GRAND: Not more. Almost as many, though.

MAGDA: Can you drive a truck or a bus?

GRAND: I used to think so, once. But it's very hard, keeping that much machinery working toward the same end. Or even together.

MAGDA: Where did you get this car?

GRAND: Oh, it was around. Cars like this were quite popular some years ago.

MAGDA: No, but I mean where did you get it?

GRAND: I told you; it was . . . well . . . simply around. It was available.

MAGDA: *(a little disbelieving)* Just around?

GRAND: That's right.

MAGDA: *(astonished)* You mean you just found it?

GRAND: That's right.

MAGDA: Do people just find these things?

GRAND: Most do. Some, of course, build them themselves.

MAGDA: *(firmly)* I don't believe it.

GRAND: *(gently)* You don't have to. You'll understand that, later.

MAGDA: *(pouting)* But nobody has a car like this one anymore.

65

GRAND: I don't see what difference that makes.

MAGDA: Well I don't want to ride in this heap anymore.

GRAND: *(a little angry)* Nevertheless, you'll just have to stick with it for a while longer.

MAGDA: But why? Why do I have to stick with it if I don't want to?

GRAND: We've discussed this before, Magda, and you know the reason. You've got to help me stay awake.

MAGDA: *(a slightly hysterical note creeping into her tone)* But what if I just don't want to anymore? What if I refuse? Huh? What if I just won't do it . . .

GRAND: Calm down, Magda. Have some sense.

MAGDA: *(shouting now)* I don't want to have any sense! Maybe I don't even want to go to the city anymore! Why do I have to stay in this old, old car . . .

GRAND: Magda, stop it! Keep your hands off my arms; I can't drive that way!

MAGDA: Well then stop and we'll have a rest! And look at the trees! And maybe meet people! And . . .

GRAND: We haven't time for that. Let go of my arm!

MAGDA: Look at me! Look at me for once! Just for once, take the time to . . .

GRAND: If I don't keep my eyes on the road you won't be around to look at! Magda! I said let go of my arm! I can't . . .

MAGDA: I don't care, I don't care, I just want to get off this road and make some friends and stop moving all the time and . . .

GRAND: *(raising his voice)* Magda! Take your arm off the steering wheel! *(struggling)* You silly fool! We're going off the road! . . .

MAGDA: Well then let's go off the road, let's get off and . . .

66

GRAND: *(yelling)* Magda!!

With a hollow popping of gravel and squeals of rubber, the back end of the old sedan breaks away, fish-tailing across the road and slamming with a heavy thud into the opposite ditch. An exclamation of steam erupts from the radiator grill; doors burst open and slam against the sedan body, showering flakes of paint. Air hisses from two ruptured tires.

When the noise of the crash has subsided:

MAGDA: Grandfather! Grandfather, are you alright?
GRAND: *(ignoring the question)* Did you see the sign?
MAGDA: Sign?
GRAND: Just as we went off the road. I'm sure I saw it this time. "40 MILES TO REVELL RIVER"

*   *   *

The hospital is a brisk, low-ceilinged affair, droning with an all-pervasive sound mix of low conversation, humming electric appliances, muffled typewriters, exchanges between nurses and patients and the occasional muted gong of the P.S. system preceding messages: "Dr. White please; Dr. White wanted in Ward 9". Pale green curtains hang before the barred windows, lifting slightly in the breeze of the swinging main door.

As the young girl opens her eyes, she feels restraining bandages on her chest and arm. The old man lies in the adjacent bed, his eyes closed.

MAGDA: Grandfather, are you still asleep?
GRAND: No, child.
MAGDA: What hospital is this?
GRAND: *(wearily)* I have no idea, my dear.

67

MAGDA: Grandfather, are we supposed to be in here?

GRAND: Well, I suppose they put us in this room because they feel people shouldn't be running around with their bodies in separate pieces.

MAGDA: You've always managed all right without this, haven't you?

GRAND: Pretty well. At any rate, I've never been in a place like this for any length of time.

MAGDA: Two of my ribs are broken, Grandfather. It's hard to move.

GRAND: *(startled)* You can't move?

MAGDA: I don't think so.

GRAND: Not even a little bit?

MAGDA: Maybe. I'll try, I guess.

GRAND: We've got to keep moving! Maybe I'll carry you, I could try that . . .

MAGDA: Couldn't we stay here for awhile? I mean, there might be someone here we could get a ride with later.

GRAND: I don't like a lot of people. And besides, we haven't the time to wait until someone else shows up. We've got to go on now. We're expected.

MAGDA: I don't care about being expected. I want to meet people right here.

GRAND: Too many people clutter up the universe.

MAGDA: That's not . . . oh, here comes somebody . . .

NURSE: *(breezily)* Well, well, how are we doing here? Any problems at all?

GRAND: No.

MAGDA: Ah . . . I guess not . . .

NURSE: No?

GRAND: No.

68

NURSE: Well, I must say. Hmm. Let's have a look at you, young lady. Hmm . . . What's this? No arm? No arm at all?

MAGDA: No, I guess not.

NURSE: *(impatiently)* Well, where is it?

GRAND: *(somewhat acidly)* Out in the real world, miss, one occasionally loses these things . . .

NURSE: And why are you here?

MAGDA: We had an accident. At least, that's what they appear to call it here.

NURSE: *(indignant)* But an arm! To come in here without an arm! I do say, what an extraordinary thing!

GRAND: We would appreciate your leaving now, Miss.

NURSE: *(baffled, hurt)* Leave? Indeed? Well I must say, what an extraordinary thing!

She leaves in a huff, slamming the door. The old man sighs and sits up in his bed.

GRAND: We've got to be careful; I don't want them to give us any of those artificial arms or fingers or things like that.

MAGDA: Are you going to carry me?

GRAND: I'll try. Let me just find my shirt. Here, now hold onto this table while I get myself straightened out.

MAGDA: Your keys.

GRAND: I've got them. Always carry them on my person . . . Now hold onto my shoulder and we'll make out fine . . .

As they struggle toward the door, brisk footsteps approach the room. A white-jacketed man enters and looks around.

DOCTOR: *(loudly)* I dare say! What's this, may I ask!

MAGDA: Oh, are you a doctor?

69

DOCTOR: You might say I am. What are you doing out of bed, may I ask?

GRAND: We're leaving.

DOCTOR: Have you been released? Have you your papers?

GRAND: Of course.

DOCTOR: And may I see them please?

GRAND: Certainly, they're here in my wallet. *(He rummages through.)* Here they are.

DOCTOR: Hmm . . . hmm . . . *(becomes indignant)* But this won't do! This won't do at all! These papers are from another organization altogether. We don't accept documents from our competitors.

GRAND: *(firmly)* We have to go, doctor.

DOCTOR: I'm afraid I can't allow this, my good man. Until you get the proper papers, get back into bed and sleep.

GRAND: Well, when can we get them? And where?

DOCTOR: Oh, quite soon. From the desk on the Mezzanine Floor. It won't take all that long. Don't forget to sleep now! *(His footsteps recede down the corridor.)*

MAGDA: He's gone, Grandfather.

GRAND: We're going too, Magda. Hold onto my arm.

*   *   *

For a long time: nothing but the hiss and whine of tires on pavement. A faint growl from the exhaust. Occasionally, querulous squeaks of springs and loose screws as the vehicle jounces over dips and bumps in the road.

Finally:

GRAND: You're so quiet, child.

MAGDA: That climb down the stairs was awful, Grandfather.

The top part of my body seemed to be grating so badly on the lower part.

GRAND: That's not so uncommon, child. *(short pause)* Are you really lonely?

MAGDA: *(expressionless)* Yes.

GRAND: I was hoping you'd say no.

MAGDA: No.

GRAND: We can't be that far. We'll be there before long.

MAGDA: Yes.

GRAND: All that time. *(encouragingly)* Are you excited!

MAGDA: *(raising her voice)* Yes I'm excited!

GRAND: *(calmly)* That's good.

MAGDA: *(still shouting)* Yes I'm excited!

GRAND: *(same as before)* That's good.

MAGDA: *(calm again)* There's a police car behind us.

GRAND: *(calmly)* I've seen it.

MAGDA: He's blinking his light.

GRAND: It seems some people feel compelled to do such things.

A squad car, its top light flashing sharply, bears down on the old sedan. When it becomes apparent that the sedan's driver has no intentions of stopping, the officer turns on his siren and operates the megaphone on his roof: "Attention. Attention. This is a police order! Pull over to the roadside and halt your vehicle! Repeat: Pull over to the roadside and halt your vehicle! Refusal to do so will result in your arrest on charges of resisting the law!"

MAGDA: *(a little worried)* Grandfather, he's pulled alongside!

GRAND: *(shouting)* That just means we're even, child! Nothing to worry about!

MAGDA: *(afraid)* He's squeezing us off the road!

GRAND: *(peeved)* Damn! I suppose we'll have to stop after all.

MAGDA: Stop, Grandfather; he's going to hit us if you don't!

GRAND: These one-track minded fools!

He pulls the sedan to the shoulder and slows down. The squad car does the same. When the two cars come to a standstill on the gravel the officer approaches the sedan and knocks on the window, his note pad in his hand. The old man opens the vent.

OFFICER: *(in a clipped, staccato monotone)* Name?

GRAND: Grandfather.

OFFICER: Spelled with "t" or "d"?

GRAND: "d".

OFFICER: Destination?

MAGDA: The city.

OFFICER: That right, Mr. Grandfather?

GRAND: That's right.

OFFICER: Please answer all questions by yourself in the future, Mr. Grandfather. You have a license?

GRAND: I'm afraid not. That is, I had one, but it expired as far as I know.

OFFICER: Insurance?

GRAND: No.

OFFICER: Registration?

GRAND: No.

OFFICER: Your license plates are many years behind; you don't have any new ones?

GRAND: No.

OFFICER: Present age?

GRAND: *(suddenly uncertain, stuttering)* Well now . . . as for that . . . I mean, a man's got to . . . I mean, you

remember too many things and . . . I've never really
thought . . .

OFFICER: *(also stuttering, quickly)* Ah, Mr. Grandfather . . .
sorry I . . . ah . . . now just a minute, there's . . . well
according to . . . I mean you don't have to . . .
(suddenly shouting loudly) MARRIED?

GRAND: *(immediately calm)* No.

OFFICER: *(same)* Children?

GRAND: Five.

OFFICER: Ages?

GRAND: Sorry, no idea.

OFFICER: This girl?

GRAND: My niece.

OFFICER: Age?

GRAND: Young.

OFFICER: Color of hair?

GRAND: Black.

MAGDA: *(whispering loudly)* But it's blond, Grandfather!

GRAND: *(reasserting)* Black!

OFFICER: I heard you, Mr. Grandfather. Own any property?

GRAND: Farm on the other side of the line.

OFFICER: This car?

GRAND: Found.

OFFICER: Any complaints?

GRAND: Lights don't work at night.

OFFICER: Be driving into town tonight?

GRAND: Could be.

OFFICER: . . . ah . . . em . . . ah . . . you're self-employed?

GRAND: That's right.

OFFICER: *(stutters in an aimless way, having run out of
questions)* . . . ah . . . you . . . I mean . . . Now let's see . . .

GRAND: *(suddenly very sharply)* OFFICER!

73

OFFICER: *(instantly calm)* Sir!

GRAND: Age?

OFFICER: Forty, sir!

GRAND: Married?

OFFICER: Yes, sir!

GRAND: Children?

OFFICER: Five, sir!

GRAND: Domicile?

OFFICER: Hereford City, sir!

GRAND: Destination?

OFFICER: Back home, sir!

GRAND: Proceed, corporal!

OFFICER: Thank you, sir!

He leaves, folding his notepad into his pocket. As his car spins its wheels on the gravel:

MAGDA: There he goes, on his way home now . . . maybe to his wife . . . and kids . . . maybe they've got a dog, too . . .

GRAND: It won't do him any good.

MAGDA: Maybe he'll stop in for a drink with some friends.

GRAND: It still won't change anything. A man can drink forever with his friends; it doesn't get him anywhere.

MAGDA: What difference does that make?

GRAND: A man who makes his living stopping people forgets he stops himself as well. Let's get going.

MAGDA: *(suddenly)* Grandfather, look! We've stopped right beside that sign again!

GRAND: Sign? *(startled)* Did you say sign?

MAGDA: *(wearily)* That's what I said. Right there, to the right. "40 MILES TO REVELL RIVER".

*   *   *

For a long time: nothing but the hiss and whine of tires on pavement. A faint growl from the exhaust. Occasionally, querulous squeaks of springs and loose screws as the vehicle jounces over dips and bumps in the road.

Finally:

MAGDA: Grandfather, are there always a lot of little towns
    before the city?
GRAND: Usually.
MAGDA: Why do people need little towns?
GRAND: Well . . . maybe to get used to the idea of the city
    I guess.
MAGDA: *(musingly)* Little towns are made up of gas
    stations, motels and cafes.
GRAND: Little towns don't believe in themselves, child.
    Everyone just passes through.
MAGDA: But people don't run much in a town.
GRAND: There's no real place to go.
MAGDA: You always talk about going someplace.
GRAND: You've got to have someplace to go.
MAGDA: Look, Grandfather; those people over there by that
    farmhouse.
GRAND: I can't always look, Magda; I'm driving.
MAGDA: They're having a picnic. Out under those trees.
    And they've got a whole bunch of cows.
GRAND: Yes, well . . .
MAGDA: *(dreamily)* I'd like to sit out there on that field and
    chew grass with those cows for a hundred years . . .
GRAND: If you'd keep your mind on where you're going, you
    wouldn't be wishing those silly things.
MAGDA: *(not listening)* Or maybe be a chicken . . . only;

75

have to lay one single egg a day, and then the rest of the
day is free. . . .

GRAND: Or maybe be a cabbage eh? All you'd have to do all
day is just be there and do nothing.

MAGDA: No, not a cabbage . . . they cook those . . .

Suddenly, without warning, the engine in the old sedan begins
to stutter, then cough and spit. The old man quickly rams
down on the clutch, trying to rectify whatever is troubling his
machine by racing it in short, stiff spurts. The coughing only
becomes worse. The old man's face creases with worry; he pulls
every lever and button he can think of, shifts to a lower gear,
hastily scans the instrument panel for an answer; nothing. The
engine stops pulling; they roll down a slight incline in the road
toward a service station, the old man still trying desperately to
keep the motor alive. It kicks over a few times more, then
falters and dies as they roll into the station. The old man waves
to the station attendant, his face now a conflicting interplay of
hope and fear:

ATTENDANT: Yes sir?

GRAND: We seem to be having a bit of trouble with the
carburetor; can you have a look at it right away?

ATTENDANT: (looking doubtfully at the old sedan) Well,
I suppose we can give it a try. Just pull into that stall on
your right.

MAGDA: That mechanic looks awfully young, Grandfather.

GRAND: People grow up with cars these days, child. Get
them at a younger and younger age.

MAGDA: Do they drive when they're that young?

GRAND: Many of them do.

MAGDA: Don't they smash up a lot of cars?

76

GRAND: Oh yes, they destroy quite a few, but then when you're that age, new or different cars seem to be a lot easier to come by.

A loud pop of back-firing gasses interrupts them from the stall where the mechanic is working on the old man's car. His muffled oath follows, then silence. The old man walks toward him apprehensively:

GRAND: Was that my carburetor by any chance?

ATTENDANT: *(poking his head out from under the hood)* I'm afraid that's right.

GRAND: Well what have you done to it? What are you doing to my car?

ATTENDANT: *(sullenly apologetic)* I couldn't help it sir; it's such an old contraption. It doesn't work on the same principle as the newer ones do.

GRAND: What do you mean, doesn't work on the same principle?

ATTENDANT: Old things like these tend to come apart at the ends, sir. New things these days come apart in the middle.

GRAND: *(ominously)* Well, can you fix it?

ATTENDANT: I'm afraid that's impossible, sir. It's such an old piece of machinery, like I said. Nobody stocks these old things any more.

GRAND: And you're telling me, then, that I'll have to scrap this whole car just because you can't come up with another carburetor to fit this one?

ATTENDANT: I'm sorry sir.

GRAND: *(shouting furiously)* This is unbelievable! I've never seen a country living on such an easy principle of waste! An entire car because a carburetor doesn't fit! Simply absurd!!

ATTENDANT: I'm very sorry, sir.

GRAND: *(mimicking furiously)* "I'm very sorry, sir." How comforting! And how do you expect us to keep going, may I ask?

ATTENDANT: There's a bus depot just a quarter of a mile down the road, sir. Pretty well in the middle of town.

GRAND: A bus! A bus!

MAGDA: Grandfather, please. Let's take a bus.

GRAND: A bus! Did you hear that? I, who have been driving my own four wheels for years and years, I'm supposed to take a bus!

MAGDA: Grandfather, you could use a rest, you've been driving ever since I can remember.

GRAND: I don't need any rest. I'm as fit as anyone; I can drive.

MAGDA: Why don't we just take a bus to the city this one time? Then you can get yourself another car when we get there.

(A short pause: Grandfather hesitates)

GRAND: You . . . you don't know what you're talking about, child. You don't know what you're talking about.

MAGDA: But . . .

ATTENDANT: The bus depot's just down the street, like I was saying, sir. I've got to go now, sorry again for the trouble.

GRAND: That miserable little . . . And how do you suppose we'll get there? You can't even walk anymore, can you?

MAGDA: We'll take a taxi.

GRAND: *(disgusted)* A taxi! A hack driver!

MAGDA: Grandfather, you're just making things worse for yourself.

GRAND: You don't know what you're talking about, Magda. You're just glad you can get on a bus.

78

MAGDA: Let's go, Grandfather.

* * *

In the bus depot, the litter, battered suitcases and waiting passengers are generally indistinguishable from one another. A directionless confusion wallows everywhere; people fall over each other, pushing and shoving into and through the queues which extend from the ticket counter, the washrooms and the concession stand. The benches are sticky with old chewing gum and half-eaten candy, heavily scarred and slashed by penknives and steel-tipped suitcase corners. Bawling children, shouting adults and the insistent P.A. system announcements give the place the semblance of a cattle auction.

MAGDA: Grandfather, we've got to hurry; we need tickets!

GRAND: I hate this place!

MAGDA: There's the information booth. Let's go. — Excuse me, Ma'am, when does the bus to the city leave?

INFO. CLERK: *(in a monotonous, grating voice)* Midnight, Bus number 3, Bay 7, Ma'am.

MAGDA: Thanks. Where do we get the tickets?

INFO. CLERK: Round the corner, Ma'am.

MAGDA: Thanks. Let's go, Grandfather.

GRAND: I hate this place.

CLERK: Next!

MAGDA: Two tickets to the city on the bus.

CLERK: Adults?

GRAND: One child, one adult.
            (together)

MAGDA: Two adults, that's right.

CLERK: *(annoyed)* Well, which is it?

MAGDA: *(firmly)* Two adults.

79

CLERK: That'll be thirty dollars, please.

MAGDA: Pay her, Grandfather.

CLERK: Your tickets, Ma'am. Bus number 3 leaves from Bay 7 in a few minutes. Please board immediately.

MAGDA: Thanks. Bay number 7, Grandfather.

Outside, the clutter of passengers and bags becomes coated with a pale neon glaze; chance movements are caught and momentarily transfixed by the flash of passing headlights, metal objects flare for an instant under toplights, splitting brilliant irises of light across the dark wall at the end of the entrance bays, then extinguish abruptly. Diesel fumes drift moodily across the haze of murky fluorescence; the harsh rasping of huge bus engines makes speech difficult.

MAGDA: *(her voice rising above the noise)* Over there, Grandfather! Bay number 7!

GRAND: *(slightly irritated)* I can see that, child.

MAGDA: Call me Magda, Grandfather.

GRAND: I don't see any difference.

MAGDA: Please, Grandfather.

DRIVER: Going to the city?

MAGDA: That's right.

DRIVER: Your tickets, please.

MAGDA: Here they are.

DRIVER: Thank you Ma'am. *(punches ticket)* Can I help you get up?

MAGDA: Would you, please?

DRIVER: Certainly. Especially for such a beautiful young lady.

MAGDA: *(frankly pleased)* Why thank you.

DRIVER: Don't thank me, Ma'am. Now up this step here . . . easy . . . there we are.

80

GRAND: We'd like to have the seat right behind the driver's seat, please.

DRIVER: We'll see what we can do for you, sir. Yes, it looks like seats 1A and 1B are still vacant.

GRAND: We'll take them.

MAGDA: I want the one beside the window, Grandfather.

GRAND: Certainly. There you are.

DRIVER: *(into P.A. system)* Good evening, ladies and gents. We welcome you aboard the City-bound Express. We hope you will be comfortable and will enjoy your trip. Thank you. *(P.A. system clicks off)*

The door slams shut with a decisive thump. Racing his engine in short, stiff spurts, the driver meshes the huge, chattering teeth of the diesel's transmission into reverse and heaves on the steering wheel. The bus glides slowly out of the bay, exit and signal lights flashing.

MAGDA: Gosh the inside of this bus is lovely! And so cool.

DRIVER: We have excellent air-conditioners, Ma'am.

GRAND: Excuse me, Driver; how many cylinders does this diesel have?

DRIVER: Six, sir.

GRAND: Pretty big?

DRIVER: Reasonably large, sir.

GRAND: This bus in pretty good shape otherwise? I mean, it's made to carry a lot of people, safely?

DRIVER: We try to keep our buses in good repair, sir.

GRAND: I mean, when you've got so many different people in one bus, it gets kind of hard to please them all, doesn't it?

DRIVER: Most people use our facilities because they want to, Mr. . . .

GRAND: Grandfather.

DRIVER: Mr. Grandfather. If they aren't satisfied, they transfer over to our competitors. We try not to let that happen.

GRAND: *(confidentially)* You see, I've never had to use a bus before, like this. I've always had my own car.

DRIVER: Not everyone can afford that. Not everyone has the ability, either.

GRAND: No, I know. But do you find that of the people who drive with you, most are too young or too old to drive?

DRIVER: Oh, by no means. Many in this bus could drive if they really wanted to. If they had a mind to.

GRAND: Well, why don't they?

DRIVER: Some find it more relaxing to drive with us; steering a car through traffic can be a hectic job. Some are simply too tired at the end of a hard day's work at the factory. And of course there are the lazy ones, sometimes quite a few of those. Why are you driving with us, Mr. Grandfather?

GRAND: My car broke down.

DRIVER: Well yes, that happens quite often too.

*　　*　　*

For a long time: nothing but the hiss and whine of tires on pavement. A faint growl from the exhaust. Occasionally, querulous squeaks of springs and loose screws as vehicle jounces over dips and bumps in the road. Finally:

DRIVER: *(over P.A. system)* Ladies and gents, I'm very sorry to have to announce that we will be obliged to make an approximately six hour stop in Clareville for vehicle servicing and a few other miscellaneous details that require some attention. *(P.A. system clicks off)*

MAGDA: Grandfather!

GRAND: Mmm . . .

MAGDA: Grandfather, wake up! We're stopping in town for six hours!

GRAND: *(waking slowly)* Mmmm . . . What? What did you say?

MAGDA: We're stopping in this Clareville for six hours.

GRAND: Was this on the itinerary? I don't recall it.

MAGDA: I don't think so.

GRAND: Strange. And what a blasted nuisance! *(addresses Driver)* Mr. Driver, is this a regular stop?

DRIVER: We don't often make it, Mr. Grandfather, but tonight I'm afraid it can't be helped.

GRAND: Well is there any particular reason? Anything wrong with the bus?

DRIVER: Oh nothing to get excited about, Mr. Grandfather.

GRAND: I don't understand it. We'll get to the city much later than we planned . . . outrageous, that's what it is . . . can't they keep their buses properly serviced on the road? Well, don't say I didn't warn you. . . .

MAGDA: Oh look, Grandfather, a huge old church! Let's go see it while we're here. That'll give us something to do for six hours.

GRAND: It's probably quite far from the depot.

MAGDA: But we've got six hours.

GRAND: All that walking . . . oh well, all right, all right.

MAGDA: *(to Driver)* Won't you help me out, sir?

DRIVER: Of course; at your service, Ma'am.

MAGDA: Thank you; is it far to that old church we saw as we came into town?

DRIVER: Well it is quite far, actually, yes.

MAGDA: I want to go anyway, Grandfather. Is it down this
  street?
DRIVER: Yes, just follow it to the intersection at the bottom
  of the hill. Then turn left.
MAGDA: Thank you, sir.
DRIVER: A pleasure, Ma'am.

Leaving the mottled glare of Clareville's bus depot, the two
begin to make their way down the steep cobblestone alleys of
the town toward the church spire, visible almost in its entirety
even from the depot. The streets glisten with the sweat of recent
rain; a faint night wind floats thinly among the dark buildings;
few windows show any light at all and even the streetlamps
seem unusually dim.

MAGDA: Grandfather, this town looks awfully empty.
GRAND: I've just been noticing that.
MAGDA: No people anywhere.
GRAND: No cars.
MAGDA: Just lights, blinking on and off.
GRAND: There's a restaurant across the street.
MAGDA: It looks empty too. Do you suppose the church will
  be empty.
GRAND: I have no idea.
MAGDA: What do you think?
GRAND: I think there will be lots of people there.
MAGDA: But not everybody. Where are the rest then?
GRAND: Maybe someone's holding a speech somewhere in a
  big building.
MAGDA: I can't see any cars anywhere at all. Not even
  parked.
GRAND: They have parking lots. And parking meters.
MAGDA: Nobody's using them.

84

GRAND: They have buses. At the depot.

MAGDA: Maybe they don't make cars anymore. Maybe they're not allowed anymore.

GRAND: It was a big depot. Awfully big for such a small town.

MAGDA: *(suddenly excited)* Look; Isn't that one? Over there!

GRAND: *(also excited)* In that alley! I think you're right! I think we've found one!

MAGDA: Well, let's go over and see!

(Footsteps speed up.)

MAGDA: There must be people here, if there's a car!

GRAND: Wonder what sort of shape the engine's in.

MAGDA: Maybe they're going to the city too.

GRAND: If the body's not too old . . .

MAGDA: D'you think the people will be nice?

(Footsteps slow down suddenly.)

GRAND: *(slowly)* Magda. That's just a piece of junk. It doesn't even have wheels. I can see it quite clearly now.

MAGDA: *(fighting against disappointment)* How can you see that far, Grandfather? Are you sure?

GRAND: I'm sure, Magda. It's just an old shell someone left there to rust.

MAGDA: I guess . . . I guess there won't be anybody there then.

GRAND: *(muttering)* Almost . . . almost had one there . . .

MAGDA: *(sighing)* Well . . . let's go have a look at the church, at least.

They turn down the next intersection, setting course once again for the spire. Their steps echo sharply in the narrow crevice of the street, so sharply, in fact, it almost seems as if the sound were being amplified in some way.

MAGDA: We're almost at the intersection.
GRAND: He said to turn left.
MAGDA: I guess we might as well walk along the pavement. It's a lot less cramped than these narrow sidewalks.
GRAND: I suppose you're right.
MAGDA: The traffic lights still seem to be working.
GRAND: We turn left here.

Suddenly a very faint noise, like the buzzing of a far-off insect creeps into the street. The young girl hears it first, stops for an instant, inclines her head:

MAGDA: Stop a minute, Grandfather. Do you hear anything?
GRAND: Hear something? What's there to hear in these empty streets?
MAGDA: No listen, I'm sure I hear something!

The noise enlarges, comes closer, but is still shielded by the high buildings on all sides. The unmistakable growl of an automobile engine begins to take shape.

GRAND: I still don't . . .
MAGDA: Can't you hear it now? There! Listen!
GRAND: *(a little puzzled, confused)* Yes . . . yes . . . I think . . . but what could possibly be . . .

Almost without warning a huge set of headlights bursts into the street, the engine growl instantaneously exploding into an ear-numbing roar, heading straight for the old man:

MAGDA: *(screaming)* Look out, Grandfather! Jump!
GRAND: *(confused)* The light! It's blinding . . .

86

In a sound cloud of squealing brakes, searing rubber and the outraged howl of a suddenly tortured engine, a long dark vehicle roars past, down the street and away into another of the town's inscrutable alleyways. The old man is left lying in the street.

MAGDA: Grandfather, they drove right over you!

GRAND: My leg, Magda. Just my leg.

MAGDA: What was that thing, Grandfather?

GRAND: Looked like a limousine of some sort.

MAGDA: Of all the dirty rotten . . .

GRAND: *(slowly, painfully)* Never mind, we shouldn't have been in the middle of the road either.

MAGDA: But your leg! How will we get back to the depot!

GRAND: *(same)* I'll . . . I'll just have to . . . lean on you a bit Magda . . . d'you think you could take that?

MAGDA: We'll have to try. Put your arm on mine Grandfather. Let's get back to the depot and all the people.

*   *   *

In the bus depot, the litter, battered suitcases and waiting passengers are generally indistinguishable from one another. A directionless confusion wallows everywhere; people fall over each other, pushing and shoving into and through the queues which extend from the ticket counter, the washrooms and the concession stand. The benches are sticky with old chewing gum and half-eaten candy, heavily scarred and slashed by penknives and steel-tipped suitcase corners. Bawling children, shouting adults and the insistent P.A. system announcements give the place the semblance of a cattle auction.

MAGDA: There's our bus! Number 3. And there's the driver, just getting in.

87

GRAND: That's a pretty smart uniform he's changed into.

MAGDA: And a black plastic tie.

GRAND: *(calling)* Would you care to give the young lady a hand up, Mr. Driver?

DRIVER: Certainly; give me your hand, young lady. There you are. My goodness, what happened to your leg, Mr. Grandfather?

GRAND: A limousine drove over it a few hours ago.

DRIVER: Oh?

GRAND: Yes.

DRIVER: I'm certainly sorry.

GRAND: That's all right.

DRIVER: Would you like a hand up, Mr. Grandfather?

GRAND: Thanks, but I think I'll manage. *(gasps as he tries)*

DRIVER: Mr. Grandfather, you'll just hurt yourself more. Here, let me help you.

GRAND: I'll ... I'll manage ... ah ... *(falls)*

MAGDA: Grandfather! Let the driver help you up for goodness sake!

DRIVER: Here, Mr. Grandfather. Just hold onto the rail here. That's it. There we are.

MAGDA: *(whispering to Grand)* The driver's sure a strong man, isn't he?

GRAND: Hmm.

MAGDA: If we had an accident, he'd lift us all out I'll bet.

GRAND: Maybe. *(changing subject)* There's sure a lot of smoke in here.

MAGDA: Those old men sitting near the middle are smoking all those nasty cigars.

GRAND: Makes it hard to breathe.

MAGDA: Could you open this window, Grandfather?

GRAND: Yes, that's a good idea ... *(tries)* ... agh ... agh

88

. . . It won't open, the stupid thing . . .

MAGDA: Maybe the one behind it.

GRAND: Yes, maybe that one . . . *(tries, is equally unsuccessful)* This one won't open either . . .

MAGDA: Never mind, Grandfather, I'll manage.

The bus door slams shut with a decisive thump. Racing his engine in short, stiff spurts, the driver meshes the huge, chattering teeth of the diesel's transmission into reverse and heaves on the steering wheel. The bus glides slowly out of the bay, exit and signal lights flashing.

*　　*　　*

For a long time: nothing but the hiss and whine of tires on pavement. A faint growl from the exhaust. Occasionally, querulous squeaks of springs and loose screws as the vehicle jounces over dips and bumps in the road.

Finally:

GRAND: There sure are a lot of smelly people on this bus.

MAGDA: It isn't so bad, Grandfather. How's your leg?

GRAND: Well it hurts a bit.

MAGDA: We'll get someone to bandage it in the city.

GRAND: It really doesn't matter . . .

MAGDA: You sound awfully tired.

GRAND: I'm a bit tired, yes.

MAGDA: We'll buy lots of fancy things in the city . . . things that do everything by themselves . . . you won't have to do anything . . . just sit and enjoy a rest . . .

GRAND: I don't like to sit, my dear.

MAGDA: Well, then maybe just walking around in the evening when it gets cooler . . .

GRAND: It's getting mighty hot in here.

MAGDA: I'm getting sweaty, it's true.

GRAND: Feels like the air-conditioning is off. *(turning to the Driver)* Excuse me, Mr. Driver, could you turn the air-conditioning on please?

DRIVER: I'm very sorry, Mr. Grandfather; it seems to have stopped for some reason. Electrical problem most likely.

GRAND: Your windows don't open either.

DRIVER: Really? I hadn't received any complaints about the windows that I recall.

GRAND: *(to Magda)* Now my dear girl, will you believe me when I say that buses aren't . . .

While the old man complains, the driver turns back in his seat and begins to peer intently through the windshield before him, easing his foot off the accelerator as he does. A short while later he appears to have found what he was looking for, depresses the clutch, races the engine several times and maneuvers the transmission into a lower gear. Pumping gently on the brake, he eases the huge diesel to a crawl and pulls off the freeway onto a narrow gravel track. A rising murmur from the passengers ripples through the bus.

MAGDA: Hey! We've pulled off the road!

GRAND: Pulled off? What do you . . .

MAGDA: We're on some sort of plaza, or something like that.

GRAND: *(dully)* Some sort of plaza.

The bus makes a final turn onto pavement, then stops. Around it, an endless expanse of concrete stretches from horizon to horizon in every direction, neatly marked in numberless guidelines of parallel patterns. Signalmen in luminescent orange jackets direct traffic, appearing in the twilight like hundreds of

90

frantic fireflies on the move. There is about the place a vast-
ness, a boundlessness which wavers between the inconceivable
and the monstrous.

MAGDA: *(excitedly)* Look at all those rows and rows of
buses, Grandfather! Thousands and thousands of them,
all lined up as neatly as in a parking lot.

GRAND: *(dully)* Yes, I suppose so. I suppose so.

MAGDA: Look at them all! That's it; we're in an enormous
parking lot!

GRAND: *(mechanically)* Driver, why are we stopping here?

DRIVER: *(matter-of-factly)* I suspect you've been here
before, Mr. Grandfather. Or places like this. You
shouldn't have to ask.

GRAND: *(almost inaudibly)* Yes, yes. I suppose you're right.
I'd forgotten.

DRIVER: Can't blame you, Mr. Grandfather. In fact, it
doesn't make any sense to do otherwise.

MAGDA: *(worried)* What are you two talking about.
Grandfather, why are we here?

DRIVER: This is as far as anyone goes, Miss.

MAGDA: *(fearfully)* What do you mean: "as far as anyone
goes"? Do we change buses here?

DRIVER: Don't matter one way or the other, Miss. Look at
that sign over there, underneath the spotlight. Can you
read it?

MAGDA: *(slowly, somewhat amazed)* 40 . . . miles . . . to . . .
Revel . . . River . . . But I've got to keep going, Mr. Driver
. . . we've both got to, Grandfather and me . . .

GRAND: I've got to admit it, Magda! I'm a bit tired . . .

MAGDA: All of a sudden? But riding in a bus isn't so tiring

91

Grandfather. We could . . . Mr. Driver, aren't there any more buses at all? Not a single one?

DRIVER: The Excursion Tours coach may be running, Ma'am, I'm not too sure . . . if they are, they'll be leaving from the far side of the lot over there. . . .

MAGDA: *(frantically)* Come along, Grandfather!

GRAND: Child, I'm afraid I think it's too late. It seems like so much effort . . .

MAGDA: *(desperately)* Well then I'll just have to go alone! If you won't come along!

GRAND: Go child. You can still catch that coach.

MAGDA: Please, Grandfather! Don't make me go alone! Come on, I'll give you a hand; we can't be far from the city now.

DRIVER: You'll have to hurry; that coach'll leave any minute now.

MAGDA: Grandfather!

GRAND: Go, Magda. While there's still time. Keep going.

MAGDA: *(frustrated, desperate)* All right then! All right! If you just aren't going to come! *(grasping her bag and purse)* But when I get there, I'll come back and get you, Grandfather. We'll come and get you, all of us. I'll see you then, Grandfather, believe me. *(as she runs)* Goodbye for now! I'll be back soon! *(she waves, turns and is gone.)*

the meeting

I am, of course, acutely interested in suicide. In this, ladies and gentlemen, I refer only to those suicides which, having been carefully arranged, in one way or another signify the final total of things. There is, I submit, nothing more embarrassing, more demoralizing than to die an approximate death, brought on by a sudden thoughtlessness or ignorance. Such deaths, I maintain, are as ragged as if they had been purely accidental. A proper suicide requires most of a lifetime of thought and preparation and can never be mistaken for an abrupt surge of sensationalism. Nor is it in any way identifiable with a fear of living, which softens the skull and renders one pliable to probing fingers. There is, I repeat, nothing more embarrassing than to die of a finger through the brain.

* * *

It is a very bright night; everywhere edges jut into the glow of lights, faces seem flooded with the unhealthy pale blue-white of neon and I wonder vaguely if there isn't too much electricity singing through the wires overhead. . . . As a whole it is much like the time I first put on a pair of glasses (after holding out at least a year too long); the street suddenly leaped out at me and I stumbled about half drunk with fear and exhilaration that a piece of glass could do such maddening things to the human eye, afraid to touch anything for fear of cutting myself or breaking off edges — it was all so brittle and glittering and a little wet.

*   *   *

But it is time to identify my position. I am standing on that exact spot where nothing has as yet occurred, where nothing (possibly) ever occurs. From this spot I will step back just far enough to be unable to differentiate between a couple making love and a couple killing one another. I must reach the spot where a man gargling in the morning and a man drowning emit the same sounds. Perhaps a man racing after another across an open field will not kill his partner but merely pass him by. It is necessary that one maintain the proper ambiguities; anything less would be an insult to possibility.

*   *   *

From where I stand it is clear that man hunts man. From here, my gaze glancing off your maze of heads, it is clear that man hunts mainly man, or, man hunts himself, always. On the two sides of anything, man meets himself like a stranger and sets his traps; when the mind tracks the body and the body flees the mind we call it life. It remains, nevertheless, that in the end every man kills himself in his own selected fashion; whether he recognizes the man he hunts as himself or another is of no consequence. ("The hunt is the only sacred activity left to man!" someone exclaims, and everyone agrees.)

Now, from the absolute knowledge of the ability to kill comes the energy of desperation that creates as it destroys.

94

Every man must have such knowledge to create works of consequence, of meaning. No one knows where the thin line which
loops both meaning and entertainment begins — we are, after
all, mostly audience. Suffice it to say that a relationship does
exist, and that the man who may never stop laughing may be
the hunter as well. There remains, in conclusion, only the hunt.

*   *   *

But the time has come, ladies and gentlemen, for the naked
incident, the shortest part of any story; the several seconds of
destruction. It is curious that few disasters take longer than
those few seconds to occur; the rest is settling dust and editorial
rhetoric, for men find it difficult to accept that any destruction
worthy of the term should not be dressed in verbal dimensions
appropriate to its effect. Therefore we have first the event,
then the newscast, later the documentary and finally the
drama, possibly man's most sophisticated nod in the direction
of incident. Into which category the following episode falls can
only be decided by yourself.

*   *   *

Somewhere, from a seat either in the audience or on the
platform, a man stands up to identify himself. He has been
sitting in this room for the duration of the meeting and is only
now being introduced. May I present to you Mr. Leo Roget,
chief supervisor of the Discuiser Group Dynamics Corporation.
(Applause).

"Thank you. Thank you very much." (Applause settles
slowly).

"Well; where do we begin? One never really knows, does
one? These things begin so quietly, so incidentally, yet so
quickly . . .

Very briefly, I am here tonight because, as many of you might already have suspected, there has been widespread dissatisfaction with your effectiveness as an audience. Your phlegmatic reaction to performers, your miserable sense of timing in submitting your applause and paying the required tribute in ovations and curtain calls has been, quite frankly, deplorable. Some of you have had the gall, the effrontery to make value judgments for which you are not qualified, others have taken to babbling the most mindless abstractions and uncontrolled verbiage under the guise of criticism. Words, gentlemen, are the fastest growing seeds I know, and many a man has bespoken a jungle that sprang up around him before he could leap to the safety of silence —

But to continue: to function effectively, an audience must be defined with the following guidelines in mind; it is, as all of you will be forced to admit, nothing more or less than a haphazard collection of tourists, of nomads drifting from theatre to theatre in restless search of the best teller of falsehoods, the most convincing singer of lies. Of such performers you must take your snapshots, make your notations on the backs of postcards to send to your friends back home. Above all, you must always laugh, for this is the expectation of the entertainer who has been carefully trained to skip between the ropes of his lines like a carefree child on a windy afternoon. Besides, laughter precludes thinking, which is the way we like it.

*   *   *

As you, who listen or read, are of necessity audience, I must assume that you have strayed into this story to confess. We will all, in time, reveal our various secrets, but in a different fashion: I will decide what you have committeed and what you will disclose. Whatever particular method of survival you choose after you have been informed of your crimes, is, of course, your own affair.

*   *   *

I began this story with a few short thoughts on suicide; this fascinated many of you but I saw some of you showing signs of impatience; do you think that the last word on suicide has been spoken? Do you think that any conscious man can afford to ignore his own death? Do you feel you have encountered all forms of suicide already? You will admit your ignorance and pay closer attention.

I followed my short discourse with a mood-piece; an over-strung consciousness slithering precariously along the wet glass rails of the mind toward the outskirts of madness. It was in some ways a self-contained piece and many of you clung to this explanation, afraid to risk a misguided connection or sus-picious of a structural trap. Such suspicions are always well-founded when groping through the labyrinth of suicides in which we are getting lost. A suddenly opened door is, obviously, as startling as it is dangerous.

I halted, then, in deference to those who cannot explore without maps; the position I defined was of necessity a relative one, inevitable in an unmarked landscape heavily strewn with deviously placed possibilities, set to explode into meaning at the first false step of the uninformed intruder. I could see several of you beginning to strain against the dark, eager to abort our investigation with immediate solutions, quick-drying answers to an uncomfortable problem. But the barbed darkness tangled with your clothes, and to have left at this point would have implied a torn appearance without the excuse of an explana-tion to offer your own audience later on. Therefore, you stayed.

*   *   *

But I must quicken my pace, as the ever-tightening inward spiral of explanations strains to overtake itself at the center of things; I came, soon after, to the largest, most point-blank description of the story in which we are caught; the trap with the longest teeth. "It remains, nevertheless, that every man kills himself in his own selected fashion." And when someone shouted: "Man is not himself only; he is himself as well!" (This exclamation, since it does not appear in the section being referred to may have been made in connection with a similar account at some other time), the raw materials, the necessary theoretic foundation, the landscape and the man were identified and set in motion. One of the man, of course, has been (had been) running at the speed of chronological time since this story began. His speed continues to remain as constant as that time itself.

It was precisely at this point, at the suburbs of incident, that I was introduced and began to speak. I took you to task for your poor performance as an audience, I warned you of the dangers of passing under a ceiling of words lacking the necessary supports; some of you were insulted, offended — I was pleased to see it. I laid down rules for those who were unable to create their own; such men I accuse of laziness, for it is easier to obey another man's laws than to follow one's own. I spoke of the beginning of this story and re-introduced the purpose of both the story and my presence.

A short scene followed, possibly on film, possibly here on stage, possibly simply in your own mind. We, all of you, became increasingly suspicious of the landscape through which we were speaking, but to turn back was as incoherent a proposition as to continue on. Therefore, I repeat, you stayed.

*　　*　　*

But I am running now. I am running, and if I pay less attention to you all in the time to come you must understand, as you no doubt already understand, that it is both difficult and unwise for a man to turn his head to converse with a bystander during his own race. In a burst of speed someone recognized the two men, one chasing the other, and shouted an explanation which several of you (I can no longer tell) may have heard. Suddenly I was introduced, I flung out accusations, warnings, insults — the story began again and a scene, barely rewound, was fed through the sprockets once more at double speed. Caution was thrown to the wind, possibilities stepped on, exploded; there was no way back. I ran, shouted apologies, raced, felt my chest kindle, burn, stared fixedly at my back looming larger and larger before my eyes; (I, closer and closer behind me and no way to quicken my pace) quickened my pace; I, being constantly, incessantly introduced, replayed, I speak (no way back) ; speak of introductions, re-echoed, aped, speak of speaking, of I speak of I, of I, speak, I, I, I I II iii . . .

*   *   *

Chaos has erupted in the hall; women clap hands over their children's eyes, a bevy of men scramble to climb the stage and reach the man who is now superimposed and motionless, frozen in an attitude of desperate flight under the glare of a single spotlight. Those of you with hands over your eyes are being hurried out of the room; those who have been here as specta-tors should quickly follow suit — I give you this advice from prior experience in these matters. The house lights, which will shortly be turned on, blind those who remain. It is sufficient that you have been witness to something you may not under-stand — something which may not even have happened. A slight resetting of the lens suffices to blur the incident into the final stages of a successful cocktail party. Critics will note that since the man enacting desperate flight was doing precisely what everyone else in the hall was doing, there was, in fact, no incident at all — merely an audience pushing its way out of a theatre which had no play to offer. A lecture audience breaking up for lunch. All such explanations are, of course, not only true but irrelevant. It will be sufficient if you, the audient, will eventually, one day, attack yourself with an incomprehensible violence, using whatever methods you will then best understand. You might, for instance, tell a similar story to your own audience in your own selected fashion. But of course there are an infinite number of other, possibly more effective methods, many of which you will recognize when your eyes become more properly accustomed to the dark."

the past people

IIIIIIIIIIIIIIIIIIIIIIIIIIIIIIIIIIIIIIIIIIIIIIIIIIIIIIIIIIIIIIIIIIIIIIIIIIIIIIIIIIIIIIIIIIIIIIIIIIIIIIIIIIIIIIIIIIIIIIIIIII

I had just returned home when I heard a hammering in my kitchen. My investigation revealed a small child, busily nailing a piece of plywood to one of the walls.

I retrieved the hammer, gathered the nails and pushed the child out the back door.

I met him again on my way upstairs. He was accompanied by a friend.

I threw them both out. Or, more properly put, carried them out. They offered no resistance but let their bodies go limp. Neither said a word.

With both front and back door locked, there should have been no further intrusions. But there was the crash of a falling vase in the living room. Half a dozen children gravely stared back as I gazed through the folding doors.

They were raggedly dressed — generally dishevelled and curiously misty-eyed — their faces quite expressionless, almost vacant. As I watched, one lazily upset an expensive desk-lamp which shattered on the floor. The other children didn't move.

Enraged, I burst into the room and began to drag them out. It was a difficult task; like their comrades, they fell slack in my grasp. And I had no sooner closed the door on them, when I saw a small child crouching beneath the table in the hall.

There was another hanging from the bannister, and three behind the couch. Another climbed the piano and sat motionless on its top.

I charged like an angry moose. But they didn't run and offered no resistance.

I grabbed one of them by the collar, dragged him to the door and flung him down the stairs. His head struck the steel railing, opening a huge gash on the side of his head. He rolled over and down the steps and lay motionless at the bottom, bleeding heavily.

Startled, I turned and ran into the house for bandages. I hadn't intended to hurt anyone that badly. As I opened the door to the bathroom I saw it was full of children, sitting in the bath, on the toilet, hanging from the towel rack and one even squeezed on top of the medicine cabinet.

I forced my way toward it, hauled it down, and opened the cabinet. There were no bandages; the children had emptied everything.

I began to shake. My eyes dilated and I could feel a steadily rising pressure in my chest and head. I picked up several of the twisted useless bandages from the floor and made my way back to the front stairs. As I passed through the bathroom door, one of the children nonchalantly put out his foot and sent me tripping headlong into a glass cabinet.

I picked myself out of the shambles of glass and crockery and became very quiet. My chest felt reinforced with wide steel bands and my head washed by a painful clarity. I waved my hand generally over the entire scene. "Get out," I commanded in a clipped, clear, equi-emphasized tone. "Get the hell out. All of you."

No one moved. Silence hung like a limp rag from the rafters. I appeared to be the only one under any sort of stress.

I tried once more, the faint rage already slowly floating up from the bottom of my brain again, my voice shaking a little: "I said get the hell out. Out. Do you hear? Everybody!"

One of the boys got up and walked toward the back of the living room, trailing the table cloth from the dining room table. It caught on the raised spindle of the record player and brought it crashing down.

Something inside me echoed the crash. I went berserk, tore into them blindly, flinging them against walls, out windows, into each other and through the open front door. Children hurtled through the air like an explosion of rag dolls, arms and legs flopping stupidly, bodies thudding into wood, glass and steel. A little girl burst through the plate glass living room window, crushing her head and cutting a deep slash into her side. A boy's arm cracked audibly as he hit the side of the fireplace where the brass plating met the brick. Another broke his neck slamming into the television set.

When I came to my senses, the house was densely packed with children. Several larger boys were picking their way through the crowd, noting casualties on small note pads, though no one made a move to help those who had been injured. Assuming those with note pads might be "in charge", I struggled through a flail of arms and legs and grabbed one of them by the arm. He turned to me, and his eyes were a glassy red.

"Listen," I told him, jerking his arm urgently; "listen, what's all this about? Who are you people anyway, and what are you doing in my house?" He stared at me as if he didn't understand. I tried again. "I'll call the police!" I threatened. "They'll clear the lot of you out, the whole lot. Throw every one of you behind bars for years!"

No response. His arm in my hand felt like a dead branch. I let it drop.

I could feel my anger rising again; thoughts of blowing the house to bits, regardless of my possessions, filtered through my mind; or shooting the entire mob to shreds. How in a civilized country with a functioning legal system, could anything like this possibly take place? The audacity, the flaming insolence of the invasion was beyond all description. I worked my way toward the telephone to call the police, but when I got there the line was dead.

I was about to attempt an exit by the back door to reach my next-door neighbour when an eruption of carpentry sounds attracted my attention to the kitchen. When I arrived, they were tearing down partitions, fixtures and cabinets A little girl pounded at the wall between kitchen and dining room with a sledge, smashing great holes into the plaster, while a boy hacked away at the studs with an axe. The wall was soon demolished and a detail of toddlers began tearing up the linoleum floor.

Seeing red, I attacked again. I grabbed the nearest child by the arm, flung it across the room and reached for another. I kicked and punched, hurled and slammed and lunged — it seemed to make no difference. For each child I injured or killed, another was squeezed into its place and in the end I was jostled more and more tightly on all sides by the crowd.

Now beyond all reason, I pushed and jabbed my way to one of the last remaining kitchen drawers and found a long slim carving knife. With a quick twist of my hand, I plunged the knife deep into the nearest child's chest. He disappeared as silently as if he had melted away. The crowd seemed to have trampled him underfoot.

There was no reaction anywhere.

The congestion appeared to be becoming more and more impossible. I was finding it increasingly more difficult to breathe; there seemed hardly enough room to expand my chest. By now most of the children in the house had others riding on their backs, and in a few cases I saw them stacked in three's. I began to fear for my life; I could feel myself becoming dizzy.

In desperation I fought my way toward the stairs and secured a hold on the bannister. Making use of the periodic waves of movement which rippled through the crowd as new arrivals swarmed through the doorways, I swung myself onto the bannister and swayed there for a moment, my right hand snarled into the hair of an adjacent child for support. Then I jumped.

I gained the top of the tall oak dresser just barely in time; the new wave of arrivals completely swamped the bannister and broke it down. The dresser seemed to totter itself but remained against the wall. I crouched and watched the bobbing mass of heads and hair dip and sway below.

Safe, at least for a time, I sit here in the damp heat just below the ceiling and plot my rescue, which appears more doubtful with every hour that passes. The steady influx of intruders has, if anything, only increased, and the heads below me are almost close enough to touch. For a while I considered an attempt at running across the tops of the heads and throwing myself out the window, but I hesitated too long and now the level of children has risen above the top of the window frame. Someone broke the bulb in the ceiling light about an hour ago, and I have been sitting in total blackness ever since, listening to the thickly crowded mutter rising relentlessly toward me through the dark.

the train

The subway station was flooded, was total movement; whirl-pools of heads churned around the newspaper kiosk, bent the railings at the ticket booth; small angry eddies of lost or be-wildered passengers formed periodically along the sides of the stairs but the constant wave upon wave of newcomers washed them ruthlessly down. Train after train hissed into the station, yawned its doors, siphoned off a trainful of bodies and stag-gered out again, windows bulging.

As the crowd grew, an unsettling suction began to increase at the entrance gates, drawing in innocent passers-by, news-paper vendors, stray dogs, singing nuns, fashion models and the occasional cripple who strayed too close to the entrance and hadn't the strength to pull back. Papers from the over-turned newspaper kiosk whirled like confused kits in the draft and flattened themselves against the station walls. I was some-where in that crowd, killing people.

*   *   *

I suppose it was inevitable that I should sooner or later be forced to board one of the trains; the vacuum inside the coaches created its own suction which confirmed the choice of those who had already decided to get inside and irresistably encouraged those who had not. In the end, no one was left behind. But this is merely an assumption; there may have been those who were more resourceful than I.

Nevertheless it was some time before they managed to manoeuvre me close enough to an open door, twist the knife from my hand and topple me in. I was followed by such a burst of other passengers that I had to assume my pursuers had been many. Once in the coach, unfortunately, all former attachments became meaningless and void, and many cried at the loss of their enemies. I must admit that I too was severely affected. When not a single additional passenger could be jammed inside, the doors closed and the train began to move.

* * *

The windows, of course, fogged up almost immediately and soon made it impossible to determine at which stations the train made its stops. For it didn't stop at every station. The occasional quick passage of blazing lights and the periodic sudden widening of sound from the wheels seemed to indicate by-passed station platforms. We stood unmoving, bodies tightly pressed together, barely breathing. The train moved on and on.

* * *

I have no idea how long it was before I began to believe this entire incident and became interested in its implications and results. I vaguely remember collecting recorded sound effects, setting up backdrops and fitting the seats from an old school bus into position on the set; I suspect that a few hours of activating the props was sufficient to erase the final traces of imitation from the train, and that I have been riding in this coach since the story began.

*   *   *

After a certain time I began to feel it was absolutely essential that I know our destination. I turned my head to the woman pressed against me on my right and asked if she had any idea what the name of the upcoming station might be. I could see she was making every effort to turn her head in my direction for the answer, but her head was so tightly wedged in among the others that she never did manage to get it turned. Meanwhile I shifted my attention to the face of a man on my other side.

This man had entered the coach in reverse and was now crushed nose to nose against another man. Both seemed to be asleep, but what attracted my attention in particular was the curious texture of the skin on their faces. It seemed to be made of plaster.

The train lurched around a curve, pressing me even more tightly against the woman to my right. Her body felt hard; much more so than I recalled having felt before. An experimental nudge at whoever stood behind me produced the same result.

There was no longer any doubt about it; everything around me was becoming hard. The silence in the coach stiffened more and more perceptibly; light congealed on the windows, the faces of those around me took on a rough callous look, then slowly petrified. Now when I nudged the man beside me he merely rattled, and his clothes crackled like stiff paper.

I stood barely moving, scarcely breathing, listening only to myself listening to myself; the sudden suspicion unfolding that my body might be hardening as well.

109

With exaggeratedly slow and nonchalant movements I slid my hands around my head and cupped it like a bowl, feeling its warm surface, its coarse hair matting, its holes and protuberances; — I rubbed my fingers against an ear, testing its resilience, searching for possible hardened spots. Then my right hand stumbled across the ridge of an eyebrow and one of the fingers fell into an eye socket. Cautiously, so as not to startle myself into attacking me, I felt about in the hole.

There was no eyeball. Just an empty frame behind which there was nothing. I probed more deeply, but without success. The eye socket had been abandoned.

My immediate reaction was outrage; how long had this socket been empty? As was I to believe, as this discovery seemed to imply, that this was the opening through which I had been seeing the world all my life? Behind which I had crouched, working the buttons and levers of my mind, the filters and lenses of my sight? And was I still there, somewhere behind this abandoned shaft, still coupling thoughts, fusing images and manufacturing statements and observations on strength of information I thought was being transmitted by it?

Then where was my present sight coming from?

As I watched these confusions wrestling about on the floorboards of my brain it struck me that if my thought processes were so suspect, it was entirely possible that the people around me were in fact nothing more than a crowd of office workers packed into a commuter train, and that it was I who was out of place, or dead, or paralyzed, or that the take-up reel in the back of my head had shorted out, freezing the image I was projecting onto my mental screen.

I began to feel the constriction of the throat and coiling stomach of a man who realizes he has been caught out beyond his own depth. Under my increasingly suspicious gaze I grappled with these possibilities, trying to think them into some coherent order, some systematic explanation — there had to be directions, notes, an outline for this story somewhere — I couldn't imagine setting myself inescapable traps, much less luring myself so far into the interior of madness as to be unable to find my way back out. For a certain degree of madness is as much a prerequisite to creation as is the creator himself, but total madness is total waste. I had to remember where the wires were cut, to return again and report.

Something must have jammed. I began to suspect that being wedged in among this herd of bodies was simply a reflection of the blockage in my own mind. With the vague intention of knocking loose whatever was blocked, I banged the palm of my hand against my head and jolted it roughly. There was a sharp cracking noise and every head in the coach jerked toward me.

Abruptly, the faces on the heads regained life, but a life which seemed completely out of control. Each face became a playground for an endless variety of changing expressions; facial lines appeared and faded through the contortions of every emotion imaginable — no single face seemed inclined or able to decide on consistent reaction to whatever it was about me that was unusual.

I felt as if my fingers were slipping off a smooth, round surface I was trying desperately to hold; out of sheer instinct I threw back my head and burst into a great reckless laugh, holding the heaving sides of my mind like a fat man holds his joke . . .

There was a furious rattling sound of steel jostling steel as the train rounded a bend in the tracks and began to slow down. Numbed, I shouldered my thoughts, clutched my uncertainties under my arm and prepared to disembark.

*   *   *

III

The steady drift of diesel fumes from the engine thins, becomes faded, finally dissipates. High above the smokestack a few tufts of oily smoke still hang like listless kites over the barely moving train; several small birds dash about them like undecided bullets . . .

Far below one can see what appears to be the flailing arms and tossing head of a man wedged in among a coachful of mannequins; the train has rolled off onto a deserted siding and has already begun to rust. Up here, where the air is thinner and less susceptible to ambiguity, it is possible to perceive the dance of a man in the arms of his own brain.

the cage

There was nothing at first. No colors for anyone to see; no shape.

Later, the flat, thin layers of day and night fell across each other like cast-off leaves; wind scuffed along the sand and bushes with the absent-minded sound of listless feet.

In this desert not even the knowledge of being desert was certain. The fixtures of desert were only concessions arranged to ward off the threat of total vacuum. Silence buckled and twisted in the air like invisible mountain ranges on the move. There was a possibility of animals, of cautious paws and hoofs on dry ground, but nothing was ever certain. The alternating currents of heat and cold loped across the land until it cowered like a charged beast, bristling at the touch, and narrow-eyed.

I was, as my father had been, a rock, a bush, a leaf or a vacuum: there was nothing at first; no color for anyone to see, no shape.

*　　*　　*

Someone, something, must have spent a lot of time stringing this bone frame with carefully stretched and heated nerves. At first consciousness I felt as if I had been suddenly dropped from some unexpected height. All around me the dust seemed to be constantly in the process of settling, and the shape of everything I did not know stretched and compressed like gaunt lizards trapped by fire. The desert wind gabbled and fluttered like a flock of new-born geese.

I came to enjoy the thin, lean thoughts I found scattered among the debris my brain continually drifted into me; long flexible strands, useful for repairing or re-weaving ornate, synthetic memories, hanging oneself, or simply collecting. I learned to propel myself through the present by simply fabricating and spinning out an ever-lengthening past, at the end of which I floated, pawing lazily through the air toward the future.

I received much, returned little. Occasionally an argument with myself, as the cave of me grew too crowded for my unruly demands. I used everything I could think up uses for and discarded the rest. I was offended at my birth and delighted with its irreversibility, but I was never certain of either.

*   *   *

Now and then, in this desert, there are people. I know little about them. Some time ago I kicked over a rock and several of them scuttled away. That was the first I'd ever seen of them. In the mornings, occasionally, I catch glimpses of them scrabbling about in the half-light, arguing and gesticulating, but few of them ever risk the brute illusion of the mid-day sun. I suspect many of them are blind.

I am almost deaf. Half my life ago I remember noticing the sound of the earth slowly fading, until eventually I could no longer hear it turning at all. There was visible movement, but no discernable sound. In its place I gradually became aware of color, bouncing with an increasing violence off the rocks and bushes; edges hardened, sharpened to a painful intensity, and I began to discern shapes that cut their outlines into the air so quietly, I could almost feel the fabric of the atmosphere separating with the unprotesting, mute subjugation of a lump of meat under a well-honed butcher knife. I kept my eyes heavily shaded in those days, until they were accustomed to the moods of a rippling desert under glass.

As I gained increasing use of my vision I seemed to lose the power of speech. I spoke less and less, hardly moved at all, only slid my eyes over smooth, grinning surfaces, groping, probing the tight mesh of molecules, the epidermal layers which from a distance blurred together to form the apparent shapes of things.

I stared for an interminable time, eventually concentrating my entire gaze on a single rock, until the only movement was the slowly sliding focusing of my irises trying to adjust to my determination to penetrate the rock's exterior. When it finally fell away, I saw exposed the proof I had suspected since first consciousness, the proof I had always felt I would find if I could just force my vision into the unsuspecting rock's interior before it could prepare itself to appear to me simply as a known quantity, a thing with a name, a category.

Inside this rock, I discovered, was only rock.

Then it dawned on me, what an outrageous fraud had been perpetrated on us all by a two-faced universe; all around me I discovered only reality masquerading as reality; nothing was what it was but was only itself in disguise. The rocks, in short, were not rocks at all, but rocks masquerading as rocks.

I remember this incident well, for it occurred again and then again, many times later, though the circumstances differed slightly in each case. Each time I made this discovery, I rushed back to apply it to all that I had left behind, but when I arrived

I found nothing left; I had been away too long; I had forgotten that one cannot safely afford to leave one's beliefs on their own even for an instant. There was, consequently, nothing to do but to retrace the entire travelled distance, it being, after all, not uncommon for a man to lose his place in his own line and be forced to begin again.

*　　*　　*

Eventually, there was the problem of fear. The fear of an empty man constantly beginning again to defend nothing at all with nothing less than his life. The fear of a man not yet accustomed to coming upon himself, without warning, in unexpected places. The fear of a man who suspects he is to himself as unpredictable as he is to the world around him. The fear of a man who knows no other method but reason.

I sat, somewhere on the outskirts of myself, afraid to disclose myself to me, afraid of the vacuum I might not find, worried that I might succeed in deluding myself and hoping that I would. I couldn't understand the purpose of the purposelessness of all my acts, and I remained confused by the lack of confusion on the part of everything I perceived around me. And yet, though I had no doubt that my own purposelessness was important, I was unable to determine the point, or for that matter the intention, of the existence of anything else in the world.

It remained for me to discover that at the base of every animal's movements, every plant's existence, every man's handshake, lay the search for water. The unexpectedly orange flower among rocks was merely camouflage, an attempt to divert my attention from the search for the water it naturally required for its own survival. The tenuously non-violent coexistence between all animate and inanimate things rested

116

stealthily on the suspicion that each was subsisting on a source of water the other might eventually be able to usurp. All around me the sidelong glances, the squinted, furtive optics of a landscape using its light mainly for reconnaissance succeeded only in creating a mirage of water, on the strength of which countless numbers migrated to the desert and died. Many of me, also, collapsed of thirst during the long, hot run toward an ever-receding ocean.

It was when I learned to live without the water everything else required, however, that my survival stood in greatest jeopardy, for a man who needs no water can provoke an entire landscape into revolt. A strange fear, an instinctive panic hovered over all that existed around me; a hatred which desired to kill by surprise and run for cover. I was forced to make a great show of clanging pails and digging shallow wells whenever I was exposed to general view outside my dwelling, and even then the rumours continued to grow that I was not consuming enough water to warrant being considered harmless, and therefore safe.

My safety, finally, came in the ever-increasing numbers of me which became evident to those who attempted to hunt me down. As the food and water shortage became more intense and the inhabitants of the desert correspondingly decreased, I began to constitute a larger and larger percentage of its population. Eventually, when I was in the uncontested majority, I began to examine the possibilities of becoming the desert, and its mirage, as well.

*　　*　　*

How many of me there now are, I have no idea — the numbers vary considerably, depending on how many can be supported or provoked at any given time. Those who become extraneous or for some reason unneeded fade without incident and reappear only where a future situation warrants their return. In difficult times it is not unusual for the numbers to become reduced to only one. In the severest of times, I have often discovered myself with my body between my own teeth.

As more and more things in this desert die, more and more becomes possible. I have developed the habit of killing something every day. Each evening I retrace my tracks, carrying some dead thought, strangled emotion or shot belief slung onto my gamebelt. Soon there will be no more interference. I have written a time into my life when I shall discover my own footsteps leading continually away from me. Where those footsteps end (abruptly, for no reason, in mid-step) I begin, constantly. There is, in fact, no end to my beginning. . . .